PRAISE FOR B.M. GILL'S SUSPENSEFUL MYSTERIES

SUSPECT

"Even better than Gill's fine first mystery, DEATH DROP, her second, establishes her as one of the best new experts at suspense in many a day. She plots her tale ingeniously, keeping readers guessing all the way, but her real talent is for characterization, and her novel is notable not only for its excitement but for its compassion. . . . Gill has a stunning surprise in store. . . . This is the kind of novel that, if promoted right, will be read by many people who don't ordinarily read mystery stories. B.M. Gill just might be moving in a P.D. James direction."

Publishers Weekly

DEATH DROP

"The best part of DEATH DROP is how much one cares what happens. That's true suspense—a story about people which compels belief. And participation. I loved it."

Dorothy Salisbury Davis

THE TWELFTH JUROR

"Gripping . . . chilling . . . superb."

The London Times

Also by B.M. Gill
Published by Ballantine Books:

DEATH DROP

THE TWELFTH JUROR

SUSPECT

B. M. Gill

BALLANTINE BOOKS • NEW YORK

Library of Congress Catalog Card Number: 81-9000

ISBN 0-345- 32514-1

This edition published by arrangement with Charles Scribner's Sons

Manufactured in the United States of America

First Ballantine Books Edition: November 1985

PART
ONE

One

THE BODY, WHEN HE HAD FINISHED WITH IT, WAS VERY tidy. The arms were crossed gently over the breasts like those of a sleeping effigy in marble. The lips, bruised by the gag, were slightly open, showing a glimpse of small, even teeth. The eyes stared at the night sky. He closed them. The clock in the cathedral tower struck one. One o'clock on an August night. A very beautiful August night. A very beautiful girl. He re-positioned her head so that it lay in a halo of dandelion leaves. It had been showery earlier in the evening and there was mud on her shoes. He wiped them clean.

Even the wasteland had a sombre beauty, he thought. The back alley leading to it smelt of someone's bin, but there was a pungent overlying smell of mignonette. Or was it her perfume?

He stood, looking down at her, strangely satisfied and loath to go.

Her name was Margaret McKendrick and she was nineteen years old.

An hour later Paul McKendrick drove his car from the hospital car park to his house on the edge of the Downs. He had saved a patient and lost a patient and had learnt neither to exult nor to grieve. He was a neurosurgeon of some repute, but was strongly aware of his limitations without being too obsessed by them. He did what he could, conscientiously applying his knowledge and occasionally hoping for, but never expecting iracles. Just now he needed a whisky nightcap, a shower, and bed. All the house lights were out. Maggie had gone off duty when the night staff had come on and presumably was in bed. It didn't occur to him to go and look. She had been a student nurse at the City Hospital for twelve months and he had taken over the role of father for twelve months, a role that the divorce had denied him during the years of custody. Janine had taken her home to her native France and access had been limited to the occasional holiday. Independence of spirit, he believed, was innate and God-given, and in Maggie's case he nurtured the seed and watched it grow. She was becoming a good nurse. She was rounding out into an attractive young woman. She was enjoying England, freedom, boys, and being with him. He felt an immense pride in her which he was careful not to show. Possessive love was a curse; she had had enough of that from her mother.

At twenty minutes to two George Webber went into his wife's bedroom and gently turned her over on her side. He smoothed the sheet under her buttocks and then laid the back of his hand against her cheek. "All right?" He had hoped she would be asleep.

Sue kissed his fingers. "What time is it?"

"A little after one. I had to walk home and I've been reading for a while."

"I didn't hear you get in."

"Good—you were asleep."

She doubted it, but wouldn't argue. Her insomnia was a neurosis she tried to keep to herself. He had enough to contend with.

She agreed that she might have dozed. "How was the rehearsal?"

"Not bad. At least all the orchestra was there. We spent most of the time on the fire ensemble and the love duet."

"First act still?" She felt she knew Verdi's *Otello* backwards. George practised the violin for hours on end.

He eased off his shoes and went to rummage in the tallboy for a pair of matching socks for the morning. "Well—you know Collingswood. He believes in first impressions." He found the socks and returned to the bed and stood looking down at her. " 'When amateurs put on an opera,' he says, 'they should have

4

a smooth start and a reasonable finish—what goes between the audience will forgive and forget.' " He smiled at her expression.

Yes, she knew Collingswood. He was a bank manager who took his part-time duties as musical director too seriously and tended to pontificate. She hoped George wouldn't come out with any more of his aphorisms. Now that he was in she wanted to settle down for the night. She had banished the clock from the bedroom several months ago, but didn't know whether it was better to guess at the lateness of the hour or to know that it was late.

He told her that quite a few of the wives had been present at the rehearsal. "You should come along some time."

She agreed without conviction that she would. It was easy to agree to a lot of things; she didn't necessarily have to do them. Being partially paralysed after a particularly stupid accident didn't paralyse the imagination. She would go along with anything in her mind—even climbing Everest. At thirty-one her mind was joyfully liberated—some of the time—and screamingly frustrated the rest of it.

She asked if Mike had been put on his pot.

"Too late, I'm afraid."

"Oh hell!" Tears came suddenly and gleamed on her long black lashes.

He wiped them away. "Not to worry. I'll put the sheet in to soak in the morning."

"At five he should be dry."

Should be? George thought wryly. And who makes the rules in this less than perfect world? "Did you drink the hot chocolate I left in the flask?"

"Yes."

"Want more?"

"No. Go to bed. You must be whacked."

He wasn't. He never was after playing with the orchestra. It was like being buoyed up on a sea of sound and left him feeling euphoric. It was just as well he didn't share Sue's bed any more. Her body looked so normal. Sexually she was normal. But her libido wasn't. It wasn't just fear of conceiving a child. A child by Caesarian section, McKendrick had said, was perfectly feasible.

5

He put his fingers in the cleft between her breasts and stroked her gently. She looked at him, startled, and he took his hand away. Since she had ceased to have any sexual awareness there were times when he found it difficult to play along with the myth that he hadn't either.

She watched him as he left the room and switched off the light. Her inability to respond troubled her. It hadn't been like this before the accident. Sex, good, strong and satisfying, had been fun. Now she felt like a pre-adolescent—unawakened.

His own bedroom was across the landing and faced the back garden. The bedrooms were too small for twin beds and in any case she welcomed her solitude. This way she could sleep naked and not have to cover her virginal feelings with virginal nightclothes.

He had come home very late.

He had a mistress, perhaps?

It was to be expected. A mistress—preferably a whore. Someone who could never become important enough to threaten the marriage. Someone not like Tessa across the road who shone with health and good deeds. Physiotherapists, she was sure, never broke their spines, or if they did they had successful operations on them. Her own operation had relieved compression on the spinal cord, but it hadn't done anything for the paralysis.

Tessa looked fragile, but she wasn't. She could lift, hold, knead and pummel. She could swim and ride and open her legs to her lusty husband. Tessa and Louis. A physiotherapist and a policeman. What a marvellous combination of strength. What a ridiculous name for a policeman.

If I don't ridicule you both, she thought, I'll weep.

The hall clock was striking five when Detective Sergeant Louis Stannard phoned his wife to say he wouldn't be returning that night and would be away for most of the next day. It hadn't occurred to him to phone at a more convenient time. When you were on a murder hunt time was irrelevant.

Tessa pulled the phone into bed with her and listened to what Louis had to say. He was cautious, not giving any details. A girl's body had been found near the Cathedral.

She said sleepily, not fully taking it in, "Another one?"

6

He answered tersely, "Yes. Expect me when you see me. You know the usual follow-up on this sort of thing."

She knew. Incident room—or were they still using the same one since last time?—house calls—hours of overtime. With luck Louis would be off the premises for days.

Glory be to God, she thought, and tried to feel a sense of guilt for thinking it. Five years of marriage to Louis had been five years of disconcerting change—in both of them. Perhaps the job had hardened him. Perhaps he had always been like that only she hadn't seen it. The word 'boorish' slipped into her mind and she let it stay there. But if he were boorish—which he was—what was she? Hypersensitive—prim—priggish? Marriage should be the communion of minds. My tongue, she thought, forms words. It isn't a sex organ for your gratification. All right—so I'm convent educated—convent moulded if you like. But Mother Ireland bred me on a farm and I know what's natural. You don't just lie in a field. You smell the grass and pick the flowers.

Oh God, she thought, I'm maudlin. A poor kid has got herself murdered. Sue is only three years older than I am and gets around in a wheel-chair. And what am I talking about—flowers?

She got out of bed and drew back the curtains. Here up on the Romney Hill estate there was a view over the city. An early morning haze touched the Cathedral spire and trailed swathes of pearl over the housetops. The tree-studded Downs, soft as a Turner landscape, slid gently down to the estuary. Over to the west the no-nonsense red brick Victorian architecture of the City Hospital ruptured the mist like an over-ripe appendix.

The other murder had been a month ago. Sally Gray. A sister in the neurosurgical ward. She had known her as a working colleague. The neurosurgical patients came over for physiotherapy in cases where therapy helped. It hadn't done much for Sue.

Sally Gray. Plain, plump, as wholesome as wholemeal. She had been sexually assaulted. Gagged. Strangled. A very neat murder, Louis had said. She had been cleaned up with her own handkerchief which had then been folded and placed under her head.

Shocked, she hadn't wanted to be told any more. "Life,"

7

Louis had snapped at her brusquely, "is more than angelus bells and the Blessed Virgin Mary."

She had long since stopped trying to defend her Catholicism. She went to Mass occasionally, but never mentioned it. She had even gone to confession a month or two back. "Father, my marriage is failing—and I don't much care." Only she hadn't said it. "Father, my marriage is failing—I want out." She hadn't said that either. She had left the confessional abruptly without opening her mouth. If reparation for her own shortcomings was to help Sue then it would have to involve far more than simply the clicking of her rosary beads. Only was it reparation—or self-indulgence? Motives sometimes became confused and sometimes it was better to let them stay that way.

She looked over at the Webbers' house. Sue's front bedroom curtains were clumsily drawn. George had probably forgotten them before going off to the rehearsal last night. She remembered that his car was being serviced and that she had promised to drive him to the administration block of the hospital on her way in. She had a couple of hours' sleep to catch up on.

Sally Gray. Efficient, kindly Sally Gray.

Twenty-eight years old.

Neatly dead. And now another one.

The sheets as she got back into bed felt cold and she drew the blankets around her, shivering.

Two

 News of the murder of Maggie McKendrick broke in the hospital just before midday.

The cancelling of the morning's operations without explanation had puzzled McKendrick's team. Paul was reliable. He was also meticulously polite. If changes had to be made his staff and the patients concerned were informed in good time. Harriet Brand, his anaesthetist, phoned his home and got no reply. Tom Halstead, his senior registrar, phoning a little later, also drew a blank. It was someone in the radio room who picked up the newsflash and passed it along.

Harriet, badly shaken, drove over to Paul's home as soon as she was free. He had returned within the last half hour and looked as anaesthetised as the patient she had just seen out of the operating theatre.

He couldn't believe it. He couldn't speak about it coherently. He couldn't even feel it. It simply wasn't true.

Harriet, picking up the old relationship, gave what comfort she could, which wasn't very much.

He said, "It's crazy. Ridiculous." He smiled wildly and shook his head. "I mean to say . . ."

She thought for an appalled moment that he was going to laugh. "You need a sedative. Can I get you. . . ?"

"She was lying there—I had to identify her—they knew who she was, of course. I mean, that's why they . . ." He paused, then shrugged. "They phoned me breakfast time. She wasn't up. Nothing new—she's always late. Mrs. Williams isn't in this

9

week—sick relative—I got the breakfast—set it for the two of us—then the phone—God Almighty!'' He took off his glasses as if that blanked out the reality of her sitting opposite him—not saying it wasn't true.

She asked if her mother had been told.

''Rendcome's sent off a telegram.''

She remembered that Nigel Rendcome was the Chief Constable. The man at the top. A family friend. All the stops would be pulled out on this one. A fleeting memory of Sally Gray came to her. All the stops were being pulled out there, too—one hoped.

There was a photograph of Maggie on the grand-piano. A very adult looking Maggie in a low cut dress. ''Maggie emerging,'' Paul had said a few months back, his voice tinged with humour. ''Maggie's nineteenth birthday portrait.'' He had added, ''Just wait until her mother sees it.'' She hadn't understood the nuance. Pride? A scoring off? He had a fetish about freedom. Just how far, she wondered, had he let Maggie go?

''You didn't look in her room last night to see if she had returned?'' It sounded like an accusation. ''I'm sorry, I didn't mean . . .''

''No. I didn't look. I never looked. I respected her privacy.'' He mouthed the words very stiffly. ''She was sexually assaulted.'' He didn't describe the nature of the assault.

Harriet looked away from him. There weren't any words for this. She had never married and could only imagine the child-parent bond. Janine, whom she had never met, had perhaps an even deeper bond. After all, she had brought the girl up.

The girl.

Maggie.

''Maggie will be coming to stay,'' Paul had said. ''She'll live at home for the first year or two. Pleasing herself, of course, as to how long she stays. It will be a time of getting to know her.''

A tactful cooling down of their own relationship followed. The occasional weekend at Paul's house became the occasional weekend somewhere away from home. He had been grateful that she had accepted the situation without fuss.

''Paul—what can I do for you?''

He looked at her blindly and didn't answer.

When Janine arrived on the evening flight the storm broke. Her agony and grief crashed around him and forced him into the turbulence so that for the first time he felt pain. Battered by words, and bloody by the hurt of them, he heard her out and then for the first time in years took her in his arms and wept with her.

She pushed him aside at last. "Where is she? Upstairs?"

"In the mortuary."

"Oh, God."

Her blonde hair had fallen around her face and she pushed it back behind her ears. She looked at him with returning venom. "You should have monitored her goings and her comings."

Her occasional odd use of English words established her presence very strongly. She was there with him. He needed her—and her only—at this particular moment. He had a sudden very clear memory of Maggie's birth. He had been present at the bloody beginning—a houseman in those days—getting in the midwife's way and holding his wife's hand.

"Had she a boy-friend?"

"She had friends of both sexes."

"There was someone special?"

"Special for a while, perhaps." Several boys had been mentioned. He couldn't remember any name in particular.

"A crime of passion—of jealousy—?"

He looked at Janine in astonishment. They were talking about their daughter. Nineteen.

She shook her head at him in exasperation and tears welled in her eyes again. "She should never have come to you. You know nothing about her at all. Girls of that age have lovers. If the parents are uncaring they sleep around."

"Uncaring?" He savoured the bitterness of the word and then spat it back at her. "Uncaring!"

She said roughly, "I'm sorry."

Maggie had not, in fact, slept around. She had slept very selectively with one man only. He, too, was in her father's neurosurgical firm, but a comparatively junior member of it.

To go to bed with the daughter of the boss man, Ian had told her, was an act of career-shattering lunacy, but how could he resist? They had played the love-game lightly, meeting in off-duty periods at his flat near the hospital. She had cooked him

11

meals. He had undressed her. They had played records. They had made love. Her virginity had surprised him. The joy of sex had surprised her.

He left the ward round that the senior registrar was conducting in McKendrick's absence and went down to the police station.

Detective Sergeant Louis Stannard, weary after a sleepless night, saw him in the interview room.

"Your name, sir?"

"I want to know about Maggie." He had once been drunk to the point of vomiting. He felt like that now. He hadn't drunk anything. "I've heard that Maggie is . . ."

"Your name, sir?"

Stannard's suave voice and pugilistic face didn't match. He looked at Ian curiously.

"Mavor—Ian Mavor."

"Address?"

"City Hospital—and a flat in Gilbert Street, number thirty-four."

"Your position at the hospital?"

Porter—doctor—what did it matter? Trying to get information was like trying to draw blood with a broken syringe.

"It came over on the radio that Maggie McKendrick was found murdered. I'm in her father's neurosurgical firm—a senior house-surgeon."

One step up from base, Stannard thought, unimpressed. "Her father has already been informed."

"Then it's true?"

"Yes," Stannard said, "it's true." He got up and pulled out a chair. If the bastard didn't sit down he'd fall down.

"How was she . . . killed?" It was extraordinarily difficult to ask.

The Press already had the outline of the case though not the details of the sexual assault—that was better left under wraps. He told Ian what he knew the Press already knew and would print in the evening editions. "She was gagged. Sexually assaulted. Strangled. Probably in that order."

Ian tried to speak, but couldn't. There was bile at the back of his tongue. He struggled to swallow it.

He remembered with blazing clarity the soft curve of her throat, the feel of her face in his hands. Her habit of nuzzling into him like a kitten, hard little bones, warm flesh. Love me, Ian, love me, love me, love me.

"Can I get you a drink of water, sir?" Stannard's contempt was barely veiled. Where was the vaunted professional calm? God help his patients in a crisis.

He didn't even hear the question. "Where did it happen?"

"On the wasteland near the Cathedral—Buttress Way."

"When?"

Stannard didn't answer. He had made a few notes on a note-pad with a yellow ballpoint pen.

Ian repeated the question.

Stannard had divulged all he intended to divulge. "No one can be sure about time yet. If you can help us to pinpoint it, it would be useful."

"I? How the hell can I . . ."

"You show concern for the girl. You obviously knew her well. We already know that she left the hospital at six-thirty. You might happen to know what she did then?"

Yes, he did happen to know what she did then. She had gone to the flat in Gilbert Street and cooked him curried rice with prawns. They had sat on the floor in the sordid little living room and eaten it and listened to folk records. She had kicked off her uniform shoes and her toe had poked a hole through her tights. He had lain on his back and nibbled her toe and made suggestions which they had followed up. They had made love on the grey tweed bed-settee and one of the cushions had dropped in the remains of the curry.

"Do you happen to know, sir?"

"She came to my flat in Gilbert Street after coming off duty in the hospital."

"At what time?"

"Probably sevenish—she bought prawns at the shop at the corner. I arrived at around seven-thirty."

Stannard asked questions and wrote at the same time without looking up. "She was cooking a meal for you?"

"Yes."

"There was a close relationship?"

"We were friends."

"You finished eating about what time?"

"A little after eight."

13

"And then?"

"We listened to music."

"Until?"

"I was on call—and was called, just before nine." In the middle of having you, Maggie—holding you—stroking you—loving you as you primly and beautifully put it—nary a coarse word spoken in jest.

He could feel his face working and bit hard on his lip, drawing blood.

Stannard pushed on with the questions, noting the emotion, but without sympathy.

"You left her in the flat while you went on duty?"

"Yes."

"Tell me what happened—or what you think happened—after you left her."

You stayed a while, Maggie. You tidied the place up. You even washed the cushion cover and put it to drip into the bath. And you drew a picture on the kitchen memo-pad with a green felt tipped pen—a couple of stick figures, with male and female created he them written underneath, and then hallelujah and lots of exclamation marks.

You're a child, Maggie.

Maggie, child.

I want you. By God, I want you. Alive. Now. With me.

"Well, sir?" Stannard let his impatience show.

"She stayed to wash up. I don't know if she stayed long afterwards. I got back to the flat at seven in the morning."

"The hospital will confirm this?"

"Yes."

"You weren't concerned that she should walk home alone in the dark?"

"It's August. Not dark until fairly late."

Stannard said brusquely, "It happened late. I can tell you that much. Was she waiting around in your place for you to get back?"

"For a while, perhaps. I don't know." She had fallen asleep in his bed once after he had been called out and he had returned at two in the morning. "Not to worry," she had said, when he had awoken her, "Daddy trusts me." Her smile had been beatific. He had driven her home at six and stopped the car far

14

enough away for her father not to hear it. Naturally she had a key.

Stannard was tapping his ballpoint impatiently. "Did you phone her at any time to tell her you'd be late?"

"There wasn't an opportunity to phone her. I was in the operating theatre with her father until gone twelve, and then another case came in which the old man delegated to the Registrar. I came off duty at five."

"But didn't return to your flat?"

"No, I went to my hospital room. I had a couple of hours' sleep and then went over to the flat at seven."

"I see. You'll be asked to make a written statement when the Chief Inspector starts interviewing the hospital staff. It will be checked against the notes I've made now. I think I have a fairly clear picture of what happened in the early part of the evening." It was smooth, but loaded with implication.

Stannard got up and went over to the door. He held it open politely. You've had two hours' kip, he thought, and that's more than I've had, lover-boy. Maggie McKendrick. An earth girl, Maggie McKendrick.

Three

THERE WERE NO CURRIED PRAWNS, OR A MEAL OF ANY DE-
scription, awaiting Stannard when he got home. Tessa wasn't
in. He guessed she was across the road with George and Sue
and went over to fetch her. Tessa had washed Sue's hair and
was blow-drying it in the sitting-room. George was in the
kitchen buttering fingers of toast for Mike.

He knew them well enough to go in through the back door
and almost twisted his foot on one of Mike's miniature cars. He
swore and apologised. Mike, with the unpredictable sense of
humour of a five-year-old, began to giggle.

George picked up the mangled remains of the Mercedes and
tossed it into the toy-box. "Sorry, you could have broken your
leg on that."

Stannard rumpled Mike's hair. "I'll get you another."

Tessa had heard him. Her eyes met Sue's fleetingly before
she looked away. Sue got the message and was surprised. Tessa
wasn't a soul-baring woman. There were no girls-together con-
fessions from either of them. Tessa gave practical help and Sue
received it. Most of the time she was grateful. When she wasn't
she pretended she was. Often Tessa sensed the temporary rejection and went away. But she always came back—needed to
come back for her own sake, Sue was beginning to realise. If
you gave alms you might have a deep psychological reason for
giving them, or you might be purely good or you might just
happen not to like your husband very much and want to escape
to more congenial company.

Tessa called out with some semblance of enthusiasm, "I'm in here. Sue's hair needs another ten minutes."

Sue's hair, Stannard thought as he stood in the doorway, seemed to contain all Sue's energy. It was long and dark and blew around her face like a storm cloud. Sitting there, she looked like a dancer temporarily resting. Tessa wielded the dryer like a painter with a blow lamp. Sue's hair rose and fell around her ears.

The room was a mess. Sheets were airing over a chair by the radiator. The flex from the dryer coiled over a pile of music books dumped at the side of the fireplace. Liquid, possibly tea, had been spilt at some stage on the beige carpet and looked like a sepia silhouette.

Stannard studied it. "A profile of the Duke of Wellington?"

Tessa blushed with embarrassment, but Sue laughed. "If that sort of thing mattered to me, I'd go mad." She amended it. "Madder."

The home-help service was cut to twice a week. When you learnt to live with paralysis—or tried to—you learnt to live in this sort of untidiness, too. Or you were good and dutiful and used all the gadgets the social services gave you and did something about it.

Mike came in and rested buttery fingers on her pale green slacks. He wanted the blow dryer on his hair, too, and made aeroplane noises at it. Tessa obliged and then turned it off. Up to a few minutes ago she had been happy. Now it was all noise and confusion and she wanted to go home. By herself.

She said almost accusingly to her husband, "You're back earlier than I expected."

He pointed out that he had been out of his home for over twenty-four hours and had been on duty for every single second of them.

Tessa asked coldly, "You're getting somewhere?"

"With the murder investigation? We will get somewhere—and someone—eventually."

He asked them if they had seen the evening papers. They knew, of course, that it was Maggie McKendrick who had been murdered?

His attitude of veiled animosity, Sue thought with some charity, was probably due to fatigue. She was the one who an-

17

swered him. George, working in medical records at the hospital, had heard about it together with the rest of the hospital staff. He had managed to get the evening paper on his way home. It was over there on top of the piano.

Stannard glanced at it. The reporters, as expected, had come up with the obvious cliché: 'Carbon-copy murder of surgeon's daughter.' He read the paragraph under the headline. 'In the early hours of this morning Margaret McKendrick, nineteen-year-old daughter of Mr. Paul McKendrick, consultant neuro-surgeon at the City Hospital, was found brutally murdered on waste-ground near the Cathedral. The murder strongly resembles the killing of Sally Gray a month ago. Both girls were nurses at the City Hospital. Miss Gray, twenty-eight years of age, was a sister in the neurosurgical ward. Miss McKendrick had just completed her first year as a student nurse.'

He tossed the paper aside.

George came in to collect Mike. "You're smearing butter all over your mother." He noticed the paper. "Any more news?"

"Not at the moment."

He wiped Mike's fingers with his handkerchief. "You're doing a house to house on it, I suppose?"

"The usual routine."

George turned Mike in the direction of the door. "I bet you can't clean your teeth—wash your face yourself—and get un-dressed by the time I count a hundred."

"Bet I can!"

"Kiss your mother, then, and hop it."

Mike kissed them all, including Stannard, exuberantly. George closed the door after him. "He takes in a lot. It's not the sort of topic one wants to discuss in front of him."

Stannard waited, knowing there was more to come.

"My car's in dock. I walked home from the rehearsal last night. I don't know what time the murder took place, but I was in the vicinity together with about a dozen people walking up Wedmore Street. I can't remember them with any clarity, but I might be able to come up with a hazy description of one or two if you've anything to go on yet."

Stannard said they hadn't anything to go on—yet. "But write down anything you remember. It could be useful."

18

"I can't trust my memory. Not altogether. I don't want to make it difficult—unpleasant—for anyone."

"Someone," Stannard said roughly, "Made it bloody difficult and unpleasant for Maggie McKendrick."

George went over to the bureau and took out a writing pad. He saw the night street as a Lowry landscape in which everyone looked the same. He made one or two efforts to write and then crossed out what he had written. Later on when Mike was in bed and Sue was in bed and he had kicked the place into some semblance of order he would sit down in the quietness and get on with it. He couldn't do it now. Tiredness, in his case, was like the over-stretching of a violin string. It even hummed in his head like a high undefinable note.

"Will it do tomorrow?"

"Yes—but don't delay it beyond that." Stannard jerked his head at Tessa. "Home. I need to eat." He saw the tight lines of annoyance on her face and didn't care. Had she been a better opponent he would have enjoyed the contest.

"Has it ever occurred to you," he asked Tessa as they went into their clinically clean, extremely tidy, little semi-detached across the road, "that the only thing that gets any polish in that place is George's phallic symbol—his fucking violin case?" He had noticed it in the hallway by the hatstand. Correction. He had smelt the polish and then noticed it.

Tessa looked at him coldly and didn't answer. His language disgusted her. He needed to eat and he need sex. She gave him both grudgingly. The tablecloth was clean and so was the bed-linen. Fuming, he waited while she undressed. Her nightdress was white cotton sprigged with flowers and she lay on her back with her eyes closed.

"Like Maggie McKendrick," he told her brutally, "only her pillow was dandelions and her arms were just so." He crossed them over her breasts. "A young couple on their way home from a disco came on her. The girl was sick. She was sick again when they got into a phone box and called the police."

Her eyes were open now and she was looking at him.

"Yes," he said. "she's dead—and you haven't even made any commiserating noises."

"Naturally I'm sorry—but I didn't know her."

19

"And it's not very nice to talk about. Sex and murder are nasty horrible subjects and I do a nasty horrible job."

"Of your own choosing."

He mimicked her Irish accent. "Of my own choosing. I do what I choose. Do you make your novena now or afterwards?"

"Shut up!"

"That's better." His mouth came down on hers and his tongue forced its way past her lips. She hated this preliminary to the sex act and had a horror that one day he would demand oral sex. When that happened she would leave. "Father, my marriage is at an end. Unnatural practices. I'm used. Unclean." But it hadn't happened yet and now he was entering her and her body was responding while her mind stayed as clear and cold as Galway Bay in winter.

Some while later he rolled off her and, his voice thick with frustration, told her about Maggie McKendrick's lover. "He says he was in the hospital operating during the vital moments. We'll check it, of course. I wonder what time our friend George got in last night."

She, too, had been thinking about George. Increasingly as her body came reluctantly alive during Louis's love-making, she thought of George. He had never touched her. His tenderness was all for Sue. His large, gentle hands tended her. He had adapted the kitchen so that she could do a little basic cooking, but most of it he did himself. They ate in the evenings, usually slowly cooked casseroles which he had prepared before leaving for the hospital. Mike was a problem during school holidays. The neighbours were good and rallied around and filled the gaps left by the social workers. She had been toying with the idea of doing her physiotherapy part-time so as to be free to help more, but was afraid of Louis's reaction. It wasn't that he didn't want her to ease up on her job. He wouldn't care if she didn't work at all. Financially they were managing. But he already grudged the time she spent with Sue. His eyes as he had watched her with Sue this evening had been sombre. He was natural and outgoing with the child, but who could resist Mike? He could, and did, resist Mike's parents. His animosity towards George—he was more tolerant of Sue—was almost palpable. "They use you like a skivvy," he had told her once. She had flashed back at him that anybody with any decency would

20

be glad to help. "Oh, you're decent," he had said dryly, "the most decent woman I know." Underlying the deep sarcasm was a seam of pain. She didn't use the word 'love' in her mind when relating to him, but in moments such as that she was aware of his feelings for her. It gave her no solace.

His hand reached over to her now and lay on her rib cage just above her heart. He repeated the question, but sleepily, "I wonder what time he got in?"

Four

How, George wondered, do you explain a late-night walk on the Downs following a rehearsal that ended at eleven o'clock? He could quite easily have been home by midnight. It had been a clear night following an earlier rain shower. The rain had drawn out the smell of the grass. The moon had worn a nimbus—a pale soft bronze like Tessa's hair. Saint Theresa. Louis's jibes, made too often in his hearing, were territorial noises, the male animal staking his claim. How was he supposed to respond? Bar the door to her? We don't need you. Tessa. Sue and I can manage perfectly. Only we can't manage and we do need you.

He picked up his pen again and started writing. Gloss over the time discrepancy. "I sat for a while on the bench looking over the estuary. There were a couple of kids having it off in a car." Voyeurism? No. But Louis would think so. Don't mention the car. "I sat for a while over the music score in my head." Why? When stress over Sue builds up I block it with any useful sonata that sings through my brain cells. Because otherwise I can't bear it. And I don't write that. Any of that. Start again.

"I sat for a while on the Downs. Smoked a few cigarettes. Relaxed. It was a pleasant night, good to be out. I don't know how long I sat. There were quite a few people around when eventually I walked home up Wedmore Street. Four or five youngsters came out of the disco. Jeans. Long hair. One of the girls wore a coat and a long dress under it. She had a bracelet on

22

her ankle." Or had she? If she had, was she Indian? Couldn't be sure. Then cross it out. Anyone else around? There must have been. An impression of people, but nothing more than an impression. My mind on Sue. Had she noticed the flask of hot chocolate I'd left on the bedside table? Had I remembered to tell her? Conversations. Scattered words. Someone laughing. People after midnight, going home. The wind had sprung up. Mike's window rattled in the wind. If it woke him he'd go into Sue's bed. The boy couldn't understand why it hurt Sue if he got into her bed. He couldn't understand why she couldn't turn over properly.

At that stage he had realised that he was later than he should have been and had begun to hurry home. Is that the sort of thing you wrote in a statement for the police? It wasn't.

What was it the police had said about Sally Gray's murderer? A sexual pervert. Possibly a single man. Someone like himself, perhaps. I can't sleep with Sue so I have it off with someone else—and kill her. Is that what they want me to write? I got home late and on the way I killed Maggie McKendrick.

He found a fresh piece of paper.

Why should I account for my movements at all? Why should I say anything? Why should I have this ridiculous sense of guilt?

The final draft was short and vague and the best he could do. He put it in an envelope and propped it up on the mantelpiece. Stannard could have it in the morning.

Sue heard him coming upstairs and pretended to be asleep when he bent over and kissed her. Her closed eyes and gentle breathing didn't fool him at all. There should be more honesty between them. I want to sleep with you, Sue, but I can't so I accept it. I don't love you any the less.

He said quietly, "I've written the statement for Stannard."

She gave up the deception. "I guessed you were doing that."

It didn't occur to him that she might like him to read it to her and she wouldn't ask.

"You explained your lateness?" She tried to level the anxiety out of her voice and failed.

"It wasn't particularly late—I told you I'd been reading for a while before coming up to you."

She persisted, "But even allowing for that . . . ."

23

"Even allowing for that, it still wasn't late. I walked a while—sat on the Downs. It was a nice night."

She frowned in the darkness, wishing he would tell her more and at the same time afraid to know.

He asked her if she had slept at all.

"No."

"Is anything worrying you?"

"Why should anything worry me?"

"I don't know. The statement for Stannard, perhaps? It's just routine, you know."

Yes, she agreed. It was just routine.

He sensed her anxiety and knew sleep would elude her for a long time if he didn't do something about it. He stroked her hair. "Will you take a sleeping tablet now, and some hot milk?"

"It's a crutch—another one."

They had had this argument before. Her doctor prescribed tranquillisers for the days when her frustration became unbearable. She took them reluctantly. In optimistic moments she believed that miracles happened and that a cure could be willed. But if it couldn't she refused to go to the wall drugged to the eyeballs. She had her mind—strong, alert, clear. And God damn her limbs. If there had to be a bargain then her mind was the better part.

"You need sleep to refresh you, that's all the tablets do. They're perfectly innocuous."

"I won't be turned into a zombie."

He kissed her. "You're a complete idiot."

She sighed. "All right—just this once, to please you. But I'll take them with water. And I'm not making a habit of it."

She didn't ask him what time he had actually returned. She didn't ask him why he had walked home across the Downs. She didn't ask him why he had sat there alone. Alone? My mind, she thought, would slow down into sleep if you gave me the reassuring answers I need. Sleeping tablets and a glass of water aren't the answer to anything.

Across the city Paul McKendrick gave his wife sleeping pills which she took with no reluctance at all. He had never seen her look so old—so plain. Compassion that had nothing whatsoever

24

to do with love was binding them together through the present horror. They could even touch each other and find some relief in the holding of hands. After the initial tirade she had ceased to judge him. Their child was equally of their flesh and the wound was equal. He left her lying in the guest bedroom and then went quietly downstairs.

Maggie's portrait was smiling at him.

He placed it face downwards on the piano.

Whoever you are, he thought, I'll find you and I'll kill you.

His imagination drew faces in the shadows of the room. His mind went on a rampage of murder. It was cathartic and necessary and he indulged it.

When sanity returned he poured himself a measure of whisky and drank it slowly before putting a phone call through to Rendcome at the police station.

Detective Chief Inspector Maybridge took the call and told him that the Chief Constable wasn't on the premises. He didn't add that it was getting on for midnight and that chief constables were not in the habit of hanging around.

"He's home?"

"Yes, sir. We're to contact him if anything comes up."

"And it hasn't?"

"No." Give us time, the voice implied. Your daughter's been dead barely twenty-four hours.

Paul put down the receiver and then lifted it again and dialled Rendcome's home number. Nigel's wife answered the phone but didn't quibble when she recognised the caller. "Of course I'll fetch him. Paul . . . I'm desperately sorry." He sensed her embarrassment. Death, he thought, was embarrassing. People went around with their eyes cast down. They shovelled away at their emotions like a river dredger trying to do a competent job and came up with something labelled pity.

Nigel's voice. "Are you all right?"

It was too ridiculous to answer.

Nigel again, "I'd thought of coming over, but Janine's with you and . . ." It trailed off. "Do you want me to come over?"

"Yes."

"When?"

"Now."

It took Rendcome less than twenty minutes to drive to his

friend's house. He had been on his way to bed and had pulled on a casual thick-knit jersey and grey flannels over his pyjamas. Out of uniform he looked less than impressive. At fifty-three he had lost most of his hair and grown a paunch. His eyes, brown and kindly, were also wary as he looked at Paul. "There's no more news."

"So your man at the police station told me." Paul took him into the living room and indicated the whisky decanter. "A drink?"

"Thanks—no."

Rendcome was glad that McKendrick's wife wasn't there. He had been bracing himself for the interview. He had been best man at the wedding a long time ago. They had married in Plymouth. It had been a windy day and the sun had shone. He didn't know why he should remember it so vividly when it hadn't been his wedding. A marriage of incompatibles, it had lasted ten years.

He sat down. "How's Janine?"

"As you'd expect. Asleep now, I hope."

"Did . . ." He cast around for Janine's husband's name and eventually remembered it, "did Claude come with her?"

"No." Delicacy on Claude's part, Paul had wondered, or indifference? But thank God he hadn't come.

Well, I'm here, Nigel thought, and I'll give you all the help and support I can and I suppose I should put all that into words, but I'm not good at it. Nevertheless, I'll try.

Paul stopped him. "I want to know what the police are doing."

This was easier. The cold machinery of police work was something he could control and handle with ease. He explained the routine. An incident room, perpetually manned. Evidence carefully docketed. Phone calls, including the crazy ones, listed. Scraps of information fitted together into a jigsaw that sometimes made sense. Callers listened to. Statements made. His training had taught him not to divulge too much, but this case was different and it was right that Paul should know.

"One of your young house-surgeons was in during the day. A chap called Mavor. It seems that Maggie spent the early part of the evening with him."

Paul felt a shock of surprise. He couldn't remember Maggie mentioning Mavor at all. A smoke-screen of boy-friends who

26

meant nothing might have been a deliberate shielding of the one who did. He felt sick and began to sweat. What was it Janine had said—a crime of passion? Mavor? He saw Mavor's long thin face and thick untidy hair through a red haze that was filling the room.

Nigel said, loudly enough to get through the buzzing in his ears, "According to his statement he was in the hospital at the time. With you. It's being checked. And you'll be called on to confirm it. It's a fact, I suppose?"

It was several minutes before Paul became calm enough to answer. He remembered Mavor being with him in the theatre clearly enough, but he had no idea of the time. Afterwards he had been called to see a patient in the neurosurgical ward who was giving cause for anxiety. A spinal cord injury was due for surgery after X-rays had been taken and Halstead, the Senior Registrar, was to perform the operation, with Mavor assisting.

He asked for details of Mavor's statement. Nigel told him what he could from memory.

"I think it's correct. I know he was in the theatre with me. Halstead will confirm whether or not he was with him. He should have been. Did he state exactly what his relationship with my daughter was?"

"He said they were friends." The Chief Constable had three young married daughters and one unmarried one who lived openly with whichever 'friend' took her fancy at the time. He had learnt the hard way that you accepted people or you lost them. He wondered if Paul would have lost Maggie in a different sort of way had she lived. Paul—the proclaimer of freedom—put to the test. "It would help if you would list her other friends. No one else has come forward."

"I can't think of a single name." He kept on seeing Mavor. In the light of what had happened to Maggie—the appalling nature of the perversion—he should be able to accept the fact that earlier she had had a normal sex relationship with Mavor. Friends? Bloody silly euphemism. Of course their relationship had been sexual. The thought of anyone touching Maggie—even normally and perhaps with love—enraged him. A paranoid reaction, possibly. He couldn't help it. The concept of Mavor in the role of murderer had come quickly—and gone as quickly. Mavor indulging his sexual appetite refused to go. He

27

wondered if all fathers felt the same. Dispossessed. The last time he had seen Maggie naked was when she was ten years of age and had slipped in her bath and twisted her ankle. He had lifted her out, suffused with tenderness. The clearness of the memory blocked his mind to everything. He was nine years into the past.

Nigel's voice forced him into the bitterness of the present. "Did she bring anyone home? Students? Staff?"

He forced himself to concentrate. The place had been full of youngsters from time to time. He had kept out of the way. He tried to answer helpfully and realised he was helping very little. There would have been more rapport between him and the kids if Maggie's friends had had no connection with the hospital. There had been one university student reading economics—very young—very callow—who had called him 'matey' a couple of times, much to Maggie's amusement. They had gone swimming together at the sports centre. He came up with his name. "Owen something—or something Owen. I can't remember."

"You will eventually. Whatever you remember, jot it down." If it doesn't help us particularly, Nigel thought, it will help you. They would routinely question everyone up at the hospital and follow all leads in any and every direction.

He asked abruptly, "Did she know Sally Gray?"

This was something Paul could answer. "As a casual acquaintance—yes."

She had been shocked and upset at the way Sally Gray had died, but she hadn't been grief-stricken. "There was a ten-year age gap. The students tend to keep together. To Maggie she was Sister Gray—one of the hierarchy. If she hadn't been on my firm I doubt if she would have known her by sight. They passed the occasional polite word if Maggie came into the neurosurgical ward."

"Maggie didn't work with you?"

"No."

But I worked with her. 'What type of cells support the nerve cells in the brain, Maggie? Have you never heard of the glial cells? Doesn't Sister Tutor teach you anything?' Maggie's voice: 'I bear a bonny bed-pan to bare behinds—the cerebral end awaits.' And he, in genuine exasperation: 'Forever—if you

28

don't pass your exams' . . . A winter's evening in his study. Maggie still in her uniform. Summer holiday brochures and medical text books spread out on the table. The brochures had riveted her interest. The text books were a tactful promise of good intentions—in the future.

The future.

It was getting on for one o'clock. Nigel, about to get up and go, saw his expression and knew the time wasn't right to go—not yet.

In the silence both men heard the swish of rain against the window. The night outside was indigo against the panes. The silence went on for a long time.

Removed by rank from close contact with the relatives of murder victims, Nigel was strongly aware now of his inadequacy. There had been other deaths. Other parents. Lovers. Siblings. For the most part he heard of their reactions at second hand. Sally Gray's sister had been down at the police station raising hell. He hadn't seen her. He hadn't heard her. According to Maybridge she was vicious as a vixen who had lost her young, only in this case it was an older sister. Her name was Rachel and she was an agency nurse. She and her sister had shared a flat near the hospital. Their parents had died some years ago. All this information ran before the Chief Constable's eyes like type on ticker tape. He could almost tabulate it. In the final column were two words, rage and grief. He saw them in Paul and he felt them in Paul. He wondered if he should mention the younger Gray girl to him and decided against it. An hysterical twenty-three-year-old who accused the police of doing nothing—who took provocative walks along the murder route—who had recently joined a judo club—or was it karate? with sublime and misguided optimism wasn't likely to be a calming influence. He had told Maybridge to have her put under surveillance for her own protection. Maybridge said it had already been done.

He broke the silence at last. "The police are extremely efficient. My team is as thorough as yours at the hospital. You don't give up if the case is difficult—neither do we. Patience is probably the name of the game. I can't think of anything harder to ask of you, but I do ask it. Be patient. We'll get him in time."

"When you do," Paul said, "give him to me." It was mildly said—quietly said.

Nigel saw his expression and, dry-mouthed, looked away.

Five

IT WAS A CLUMSY FALL IN THE JUDO CLASS THAT INJURED RAchel Gray's shoulder and necessitated heat treatment in the physiotherapy department. Tessa, applying it, realised after a while who her patient was and tried awkwardly to express her condolences.

She added, "You're not a bit like her."

Rachel, small, dark-eyed, vivid in temperament though not in colouring, was the complete opposite of Sally. Kind, plodding, reliable Sally. Raped, strangled, dead Sally.

Rachel moved her shoulder gingerly. No, she wasn't like her. There had never been any anger in Sally. Had she survived she would probably have made a plea that her attacker be treated with leniency. Had she, Rachel, been the one who had died, Sally would feel the knife thrust of pain, but she wouldn't dream of taking a course of judo and carrying a knife—a real one—in the profound hope that one day she would use it on the killer. It was a paper knife and she had bought it several years ago when she and Sally were holidaying in Portugal. It had a pretty-coloured crest and was as sharp as hell.

"No," she said, "we're not alike. How well did you know her?"

Tessa moved the lamp and massaged Rachel's shoulder muscles. "We had contact through our patients. It was a working relationship. Her patients liked her enormously. Paralysis can be very frightening; she helped her patients to accept what had to be accepted."

31

"Yes, she was a very accepting person, Sally." You took everything that was slung at you, Sally. Even the responsibility of looking after me when there was no one else to do it. And now I'm looking after you. You're not going to be another unsolved case, filed away, forgotten.

She suggested that Tessa should join her in The Mitre during the lunch break. "I've already sampled the hospital canteen and it's too frightful to sample again. You have an hour or so of freedom, I suppose?"

Tessa agreed that she had. She didn't want to lunch with Rachel but wasn't quick enough to think up a plausible excuse. Rachel frightened her. Perhaps 'frightened' was too strong: she filled her with unease. No one in the months following a bereavement was normal, but there were degrees of stress and stressful behaviour. Even touching Rachel's flesh with her trained and skilful fingers had made her feel like the student she had once been—nervously doing what had to be done and hoping she was doing it well.

As usual during the lunch break, The Mitre was full. Rachel pointed to a couple of chairs about to be vacated and told Tessa to grab them while she got the drinks. "What will you have?" Tessa said a Coke and a ploughman's to go with it. Rachel came back with the order including a Guinness for herself. It reminded Tessa of Dublin. She was, and had been for a very long time, sick of England. At this moment she would give a great deal to be back on the farm in Galway. Unmarried. Starting all over again—differently.

Rachel, with a froth of Guinness on her lips, said surprisingly, "You remind me of her."

"What?"

"You remind me of my sister." She didn't try to explain that the resemblance wasn't physical. The gentle ones were the world's losers. They shouldn't be let loose. The jungle was too hazardous for them. Even if they didn't get themselves killed they had wounds that showed.

Tessa was silent. Sally had been lumpy and plain. Good, dependable, conscientious. Nice. It was an awkward comment that could only be answered by a vague smile. She began buttering her roll. The cheese was strong and she had no appetite.

Rachel leaned forward, her elbows on the table. "I need to

talk. Do you mind if I talk to you? You needn't even listen. Just be there and make it seem normal. When someone dies you're too shocked to say anything—for a long time. And then words come back—they batter at you—they need to be said. I don't know you. It makes it easier, not knowing you. If you want to get up and go, then go now. There's a free table over there.''

Tessa thought, Oh God, and wanted to get up and go, but couldn't. Compassion struggled with her desire to flee. She wouldn't be able to give this girl anything because there was absolutely no rapport between them at all. Her mind turned to Sue. Sue, too, was dominating, but in a different sort of way. Sue, despite her paralysis, had the calmness—not always, but for quite a lot of the time—of someone in control.

You don't win battles, she had once admonished herself in Tessa's hearing, by becoming hysterical. Keep calm.

Calm. There was no calmness in Rachel. Quietness, yes. The thin crust that covers a volcano.

Rachel was thinking aloud. She thought in cameos, small mind-pictures that had no link in time. ''She had no sense of clothes. She couldn't present herself. Our mother looked younger at forty than Sally did at eighteen. She acted younger, too . . .

''She was Father's favourite. He worked in the shoe trade. Had he lived I think she would have gone in for it too, to please him. Odd to think of her manufacturing shoes . . .'' She tried to imagine Sally behind a machine and failed. The hospital environment had been the right environment.

''Mother was glad about the nursing. Handy to have a nurse in the family when you get old. Only Mother didn't get old. Had Sally been with her during the heart attack she might have survived—well, she probably wouldn't—but things might have been different if . . .''

Things might have been different if . . . Corny, stupid phrase. She looked over at the bar. A group of students were laughing and swapping jokes. Hospital jokes. Corny jokes. Sally had never laughed out loud. A lot of the jokes she hadn't understood. Or had pretended not to understand.

''She had a couple of boy-friends over the last two or three years. I don't think she slept with either. If she did she made jolly sure I wasn't around . . .

33

"She could have been born fifty years ago and fitted in. If you look at an old thirties film you see Sally. She talked that way, too . . .

"When she was a kid she saved her money and put it in a bank saving box. When she had twenty pounds she took it out and bought a bike. I borrowed it without asking and wrapped it around a lamp-post. I was all right. The bike wasn't. She didn't even bawl me out, just cleaned me up and said it was a blessing I hadn't broken my neck. Yes—blessing—she used words like that, even then." She smiled and her clenched hands loosened a little in her lap. Funny, old-fashioned, good Sally.

"There wasn't a Will, but we inherited what there was. It wasn't much. Sally trained at Barts. I didn't know what I wanted to do, but I couldn't think up a good reason not to nurse. She persuaded me into it and saw me through it. Acted more like a mother than our own mother ever did. Even told me about contraceptives—as if I didn't know."

The conversation came back to her clearly. She had teased her by asking for details. Sally had given them very conscientiously. 'It is necessary,' she had said earnestly, blushing all up her neck, 'that you should know.'

Rachel drew the glass of Guinness towards her. The froth was subsiding. The glass was cold in her hands. Why wasn't the physio eating? She hadn't started her roll. It was a croissant. Looked stale. The sort they served at rotten continental breakfasts.

"I had food poisoning," she told Tessa, "just before Sally was due to go on holiday with one of the blokes. She didn't go. Stayed with me. I got better in a couple of days and ruined her holiday. I'd have been bitter—bloody mad. She wasn't."

She pushed back her chair a little. The tables were very close. Her foot was beginning to cramp. She eased it out of her shoe.

"Sally could skate. Won a medal for it when she was a kid. Olympic material, her coach said. She should have taken more care of her shape. Diet to her was a dirty word. She went to keep-fit classes, though—for a bit . . .

"Neither of us liked the flat much, but it was the best we could get. She did the decorating in her spare time. Her bedroom was white and pale turquoise. She had a nightdress case

34

in the shape of a koala bear. She even had a nightdress to put in it. I didn't intend staying too long, but I didn't tell her. I wanted my own place, even a bed-sit, but she'd gone to so much trouble doing it up I decided to give her a year. I mean she'd been so—well—caring.''

She paused. Then said it. "I loved her. That's hard to say. I've never said it before. She didn't think about herself very much. She didn't have time. Selling the house. Bills. Me. I should have taken her in hand. Forced her to see herself. She was a person—bogged down in the bothers of others.''

The group at the bar began to split up. One of the boys wore a Snoopy sweatshirt. Silly juvenile clobber, Sally would have called it.

''The day after she was dead she would have been twenty-nine. I'd bought her a dress. My sort, not hers. I doubt if she would have worn it. I didn't buy it so that she could give it to me. I wanted her to look good.

''She should have got married. Had kids. Life is more than surviving and being good to other people.

''The night she didn't come home I wasn't home either. It was the first time I'd spent the whole night with a fella. I didn't mean to. I usually got back before she did. I got back at seven. The post had been. There were birthday cards—three of them—on the mat. I was thinking up lies about being out on a private nursing case that kept me all night. The flat was very tidy. Very quiet. I thought she had been kept late at the hospital. I began making breakfast. I was frying bacon when the police called. The smell of burnt bacon! Even when I think of it now I want to puke.

''No—for God's sake—don't hold my hand. Don't touch me!''

Tessa's spontaneous gesture of sympathy became an awkward withdrawal as she moved her hand away.

''They had put her in the mortuary. I had to go there and look. 'Yes,' I said. 'It's Sally.' I had a sort of fury with Sally, lying there, letting it be done to her. Allowing herself to be dead. I didn't know all the details then. When I did know . . . well, imagination gets wrapped up in a sort of blanket—it's muffled—and then you throw the blanket away and you see.

35

That's when you start to feel. Before that you don't feel anything—it's too incredible.

"The police were all right at first. I ranted and raved and they took it. They tried to explain what they were doing. They're like a machine churning away with their endless files and bits of paper and producing nothing at all. She's been dead now over a month. They've been working on it for over thirty days and they haven't got a single thing to go on. They don't know who did it. In time they won't care who did it. If Maggie McKendrick hadn't been murdered they would have folded their hands over their fat stomachs and sat back and said 'finis'. File it away in the unsolved crimes. But she has been murdered—and by the same bastard—and so they'll run a few more laps—perhaps more than a few laps because rumour has it her dad knows the Chief Constable."

Tessa, flushed of cheek, protested, "That's absolutely not true." She thought she had better make her personal involvement plain. "I'm married to a detective sergeant. I know the amount of work they put into every case—and I mean *every* case. If you happened to know the Lord Chief Justice you wouldn't get a more thorough investigation of the case than you're getting now."

Rachel took a sip of Guinness. "Sally," she said, "to me is not a case. She is the ashes of my twenty-nine-year-old sister. Maggie McKendrick's death has injected more fuel into the police machine and so it will run a while longer. I'm not here to talk ethics to you—integrity—whatever you want to call it. I'm here to talk. And I have talked. And you've listened. And I'm grateful."

She looked at Tessa's uneaten roll and cheese. "If I've ruined your lunch I'm sorry."

It was just her luck, she thought, to pick on a policeman's wife. But perhaps the luck was on the good side, provided she didn't antagonise her. Policemen talked in bed. Wives listened. Sometimes they talked, too.

"I can't remember your name. Which one are you married to?"

"Detective Sergeant Stannard. I'm Tessa Stannard."

Stannard. The name immediately brought a face to mind. A thick-set, swarthy man. A little under six foot tall. Smooth voice with a trace of local accent. A strong aura of underlying impatience held carefully in check. Not the sort to tangle with—except perhaps sexually. A very masculine animal.

She looked curiously at Tessa and wondered if it worked. Frail Tessa with hair like a Botticelli cherub, auburn, softly curled. Cherubic temperament, too, probably. Mild as milk.

Tessa, interpreting the look, looked away and made an attempt to eat. To her relief Rachel stood up and said she'd have to go. "I'll be seeing you again for more treatment to my shoulder."

"Yes."

"And perhaps we can lunch again sometime?"

Tessa thought—no—no—no—but smiled unconvincingly and agreed.

And next time, Rachel thought, you'll do the talking to me.

Six

THE WEEKEND FOLLOWING MAGGIE'S MURDER IAN MAVOR was due for leave. He hadn't been home for three months and had planned to go. The fact that he had first to present a written statement to the police and obtain their permission to travel annoyed him. Nevertheless he complied with reasonable grace. The police officer he had come to know as Detective Sergeant Stannard conducted the interview again. This time he concentrated on the period between midnight and one-thirty on the night of Maggie's death. According to him (the information having been obtained from McKendrick's statement and that of the theatre sister), the operation at which he had assisted McKendrick was concluded at five minutes past midnight. McKendrick had then gone on the ward. The operation with Halstead, the senior registrar, had commenced at one-fifty, which had left him with approximately an hour and three-quarters of free time. During this time he had gone to the hospital canteen for coffee and been seen by various members of staff. A closer pinpointing of the time would be necessary, Stannard had said, when he was interviewed by the Chief Inspector. If he were having a couple of days away then he had better use them thinking. Ian, thrusting down his anger, managed not to answer.

Instead of going home he drove to Snowdonia and stayed at a small pub in Llanberis. In his present mood the normality of his home was too hard to take. His father was in a group practice in Derbyshire and tended to talk medicine. His mother talked about Settling Down, the Stability of Marriage and the Blessing of Family Life. He had wondered occasionally if she had her tongue in her cheek, and decided she hadn't. It would have been more bearable if she had. He was fond of them both, but was too undermined at this particular time to accord them the civility of appearing to listen to them. During periods of overwork—and stress—he tended to reach flashpoint too quickly. Depression flared into anger that was hard to control. "Keep an even keel, boy," his father used to admonish him when he was younger, "or ride out the storm in private. If you can't control your moods, then don't inflict them on others." On entering medical school he had warned him that a good doctor needed to be emotionally stable. "If you haven't that sort of temperament then you're better out of the profession." Possibly. But he was in it and he wanted to be in it. Just now he needed solitude. He needed sleep. He hadn't had enough of either since Maggie's death. He felt raw, as if he had been kicked. He would have liked to have kicked Stannard—pulped his face in. The force of his emotional reaction frightened him. Maggie's murder had ripped him apart. He needed time to get himself together again. To become a sane, well co-ordinated individual, not an emotional mess.

He went hill walking—not climbing, he hadn't the gear nor the expertise—and imagined Maggie walking with him. It rained steadily for most of his stay. It was appropriate and kind. Factual horrors were hazed over in the grey wet landscape. The smell of death was washed away. Sodden heather gave off a bearable scent and he breathed it in deeply. Had Maggie been with him she would have been bedraggled and disgruntled—not an outdoor girl, Maggie. He imagined her wet hand in his and closed his own on emptiness.

When he returned to the hospital he discovered that Paul McKendrick had returned, too. Harriet, preparing to anaesthetise the first patient, took him aside. "He phoned yesterday to say he'd be in—that his list was building up and he wanted to get on with it. Don't mention Maggie to him. He knows how everyone feels about it. Talking just rubs it in."

Harriet looked curiously at Ian. Wherever he had been he hadn't benefited from it. Both he and Maggie's father had the same look about the eyes.

39

It was a long difficult morning. An infant with a meningocele and associated hydrocephalus was followed by a man with a spinal cord tumour. Paul, his mind intent on the operations, performed them with skill. The prognosis in this second case should be good. Both operations were performed under general anaesthetic. The patient with the spinal cord tumour was paralysed with a muscle relaxant and then ventilated. Harriet reversed the relaxant with another injection at the end of the operation. The team work as always was excellent. She was as much a part of him as his right hand. He was aware that Ian Mavor was in the theatre, but at that stage the discipline of surgery disassociated him from Maggie. Later, when he was getting out of his theatre gown, the present came surging back.

He told the theatre sister to ask Doctor Mavor to go to his room. "I'll see him there in ten minutes."

Ian thought: 'So this is it.' He and Maggie had joked about it in the past. "What are your intentions, young man? Honourable? Dishonourable?" Maggie's voice: "Delightfully dishonourable. I love you, you sod."

Paul watched him coming in. The antagonism that had been building up began slowly to fall away. Whatever had been going on between Maggie and this boy it had traumatised him.

He told him to sit down. "You've been on leave?"

"Yes, sir. In Snowdonia."

Paul leaned back in his chair. "Nice country. But we're not here to talk about that—or the finer points of surgical procedures. I've only recently heard about you and Maggie. Why didn't she tell me about you?"

It was unanswerable.

Almost as he said it Paul realised it was a stupid question. All the other questions in his mind were unanswerable, too. There were certain thresholds that couldn't be crossed. A parent had no automatic right of way. Maggie had been fully adult. If she had slept with this boy—also fully adult—then that was their business.

There was one question that he could ask. "Did you care for her?"

Ian's "Yes" came out harshly and the younger man thought in a moment of blind panic that he was going to weep.

Paul, on principle, had no spirits on the premises, but wished

40

that he had. His own calm was still fragile and had to be cosseted. He didn't look back at his companion until he sensed that Ian was once more in control.

So the relationship hadn't been trivial.

He said quietly, with a degree of truth, politely expressed, "You would have been welcome. Had she lived—had you decided to make a go of things together—I would have been happy about it."

(Happy? A useful word. No son-in-law would have filled me with ecstatic enthusiasm. I would have accepted you because of your emotional commitment to her. I accept you now for the same reason.)

Ian was silent.

A shaft of sunlight made an arrow on the dark blue carpet tiles.

The silence was strangely companionable. It was almost as if Maggie were there, willing the link that was forming between them. Be good to each other. You both know pain.

Paul spoke of the inquest. " 'Murder by person unknown.' But, I hope, not unknown for long. The police are working hard on it."

"You think they'll succeed?"

"They'll have to." My will forces success, his voice implied, I won't brook failure.

"But if they don't?"

The older man looked at the younger one. In the dark hours of the night he had asked himself the same question—and answered it. There was going to be only one end to this, and how that end was brought about lay somewhere in the future. Nobody took Maggie's life and got away with it. But nobody.

He answered grimly, "Let's wait and see, shall we? The bastard is out there somewhere—walking around, breathing, eating, sleeping, defecating. He'll be nailed eventually. I believe it. You've got to believe it. It's the only consolation we have."

That night Harriet went home with Paul. She had stayed away from the house while Janine was there. If Claude had had the tact to absent himself then it was only right that she should do the same. Now Janine was back in France and it was up to Claude to do what he could to comfort her. She would return from time to time, Paul said, but during this period of investigation she was better in her own environment. She couldn't do anything and he couldn't give up his hospital commitments for too long to be with her. His hospital commitments, he had hinted, kept him relatively sane. He had said nothing about the loneliness of returning to an empty house, but when she suggested returning with him he hadn't demurred.

The housekeeper who came in on a daily basis had left cold chicken and a salad on a tray in the kitchen. Harriet made a fricassé of the chicken in a mushroom sauce and opened a bottle of white wine. She was a quick, haphazard cook and served everything untidily, but it was hot and tasted good. He hadn't realised he was hungry. He hadn't remembered tasting food for some days. He had eaten, of course, but with supreme disinterest. One had to stay alive.

Afterwards they sat by the open french windows in the living room. The evening sun deepened the green of the grass to a dark olive. Kim, the fox terrier, sat over by the pool and made lazy splashing efforts to catch the goldfish.

Maggie's dog.

Her nineteenth birthday present.

He didn't want to talk about her. He hoped Harriet wouldn't talk about her. He felt rather like a patient on a kidney machine, forced into inactivity while vital processes went on.

Harriet, coolly dressed in a blue checked cotton shirt and navy cotton slacks, shivered a little and moved out of the shadows of the room and on to the terrace. It was warmer there. Kim came over to investigate her and she strolled down to the orchard with him.

Maggie, in the twelve months she had lived with her father, had put an indelible mark on the place and on him. It was like coming back a stranger. She wasn't sure what to do. Silences that in the past had been companionable were now uneasy. He was afraid she was going to talk about Maggie. Did he think her that insensitive? They had known each other for six years and she had been his occasional mistress for three of them. He had known his grown-up daughter for one year. Time was irrelevant. The blood tie could be a joke, or a lifeline, or a channel of pain.

After a while she went back to him. His eyes were closed and she thought he was asleep. She squatted down at his feet and rested her cheek against his knee. In a few weeks' time, she thought, I'll be forty-two. I have a bulging midriff and spreading hips. You're fifty-one and looking older. Maggie could have been our child, had circumstances been different. I could still have your child. A menopausal infant. A gift of my body.

She smiled. Menopausal insanity.

He ran his hand over her hair. "What are you thinking about?"

At one time she could have told him. Not tonight. "That perhaps I should go."

"Is that what you want?"

"I want what you want."

He felt a small stirring of anger—but with himself. "Could you try to treat me normally? That's what I want. Don't tread so warily. Bereavement isn't a kind of papal crown that you have to bend a knee to—and it isn't a bad dose of leprosy."

She asked it bluntly. "Do you want me to sleep with you tonight?"

He answered equally bluntly. "Sleep—yes—but I doubt if I'm physically capable of anything else."

The sheets had been changed on Janine's bed, but the bedmaking had been careless and a small lace-trimmed handkerchief was tucked under one of the pillows. Harriet put it on the bedside table. Compared with Janine she felt big and ungainly. She sat up in bed and looked down at her large full breasts. Seductive? But he didn't want seduction. Matronly? Comforting?

He was a long time joining her. He poured himself a measure of whisky and then another. The relationship before Maggie had come to live with him had been warming towards marriage. While Maggie was there some of the warmth had gone. Maggie had filled every corner for him—with love—with exasperated tenderness—with occasional explosions of rage. The divorce had robbed him of years of her and it had been a time of catching up. In some ways it had been an unnatural year—a gourmet feast instead of the bread and butter of a father-daughter relationship. There hadn't been time for boredom, let alone disillusionment. Her innate laziness had grated on him but perfection marred was considerably more interesting than a too-good image. She was his Maggie, faults and all, and her vitality had carried him on a crest of physical well-being. He had never felt better in his life.

And now he was tired.

Why had Harriet gone into the guest bedroom? They had always used his room in the pre-Maggie days. Did she see it as a half-way house before the full homecoming? Was she still being tactful?

Harriet realised, when he joined her at last, that he had been drinking. Her professionally trained mind reminded her that neither of them was on call. If she had been she would have stayed at home. The hospital had never been told to contact her here. They had been careful to preserve the illusion of a working relationship that ended in the operating theatre. That they hadn't been careful enough was something they both guessed but didn't mention. It was nobody else's business, but it was wise not to make it overt. The fact that she had immediately thought of the hospital—and later of his need to drink—disconcerted her. She had become a consultant anaesthetist in her thirties. She had a small Georgian house on the Downs. Professional success and the financial rewards that went with it had been almost wholly satisfying. Almost. Priorities were sometimes hard to define.

Naked, he got in beside her and felt the warmth of her limbs. He thought the whisky might have helped an erection, but it didn't. It just made him want to sleep. "Harriet, I'm sorry."

Sexually alive, wanting him, she said, gently, that it didn't matter. "You're tired—perhaps in the morning . . ." She leaned over him and switched off the bedside lamp.

Somewhile later in the darkness he told her that Ian Mavor had been Maggie's lover.

Surprised, she didn't know whether to react with indignation or with a placatory word or two in Ian's favour. At Maggie's age she had lived for a while with a medical student. He had been in an almost perpetual state of erection and had awoken her once in the night to show her what he looked like when he wasn't. She had a terrible urge to laugh.

He waited for her comment and, puzzled, sensed her mirth.

It wasn't until she had moved fractionally from the edge of hysteria that she trusted herself to speak. "Once when I was

Maggie's age . . ." She told him the rest of it—and about her student days—and about being young.

After a while he stopped listening. His body was losing its numbness. Her thighs, pressed hard against him, seemed part of his own flesh. He began to want her as she wanted him. The initiative tonight was hers and she was patient. It had always been good.

Afterwards, his head on her breasts, he slept.

Seven

DETECTIVE CHIEF INSPECTOR MAYBRIDGE WAS ALLOCATED three rooms in the administrative wing of the hospital in which to interview the hospital staff. This was a period of slog. The sifting through process would go on for several days. Those who knew Maggie would be questioned closely. Those who didn't but were off the premises at the vital time would be asked to account for their whereabouts. Those who knew Maggie and were off the premises at the time of the murder were channelled through to him and to Sergeant Stannard who was assisting. For much of the time he let Stannard do the questioning. Stannard had a quality of . . . he didn't quite know how to put it—plebianism?—which went down well with some. They opened up. With him, Maybridge, they tended to be polite. His questions were answered, but not at any depth. With Stannard they would expand—blood brothers under the skin—the sort you drank with at the pub. If they expanded too much he shut them up. They sensed his aggression and for the most part respected it and understood it. Well, he was a copper after all, wasn't he? He was doing his job.

The women staff—nurses and auxiliaries, secretaries and domestics—were quizzed very briefly. The murder had been sexually motivated and that ruled them out.

After two days of this Maybridge saw the cream-painted, blue-carpeted room as sourly as a lifer contemplating his cell. He wished some of the criticising public could sit in on a murder investigation and see exactly what went on. Even Stannard who was physically as tough as they come had dark bags under his eyes and was pale about the lips. To add to everyone's discomfort the weather had become very hot.

He went to the open window and leaned out. Hospitals, like ships, had their own peculiar smell. He expelled it from his lungs and took in deep breaths of summer air. Four storeys down an ambulance drew up in the forecourt and a patient covered in a red blanket was unloaded. Was the blanket dyed red, or was it blood? He watched curiously without coming to any definite conclusion. Despite years of police work the sight of blood tended to sicken him. He moved away from the window and glanced at Stannard's list.

"We'll see a couple more before lunch. Mavor and one other." He had been reading the notes on Mavor, and his statement, and had a pretty shrewd idea what to expect.

Stannard had described him as a lusty young stud. Lusty young studs who could get it in the normal way didn't suddenly turn into perverts. His emotional make-up, according to Stannard, was the reverse of cool, but under the circumstances what could be more natural? His girl-friend had been brutally murdered—a little trembling of the surgeon's hands was in order.

He looked at him keenly as he came in. Mister or Doctor? At his age probably Doctor. There would be more exams—more hurdles. He looked tired. His job? Grief? Conscience? Probably not conscience. He'd have nothing to be guilt-ridden about—well, nothing serious. He should have seen to it that Maggie McKendrick got safely home, of course. Or would that have been old-fashioned chivalry—or just plain impossible?

Why didn't he comb his hair?

If he—Maybridge—were lying on the operating table he would prefer the surgeon to be well-groomed. If I grow a brain tumour, young man, I'll ask specifically for McKendrick. His thinning locks won't fall into the cavity. Maybe his ageing eyes aren't as clear as your young ones, but they've seen a hell of a lot. My son's your age. He womanises, too. Discreetly off the parental patch. He'd have played around with Maggie, given the chance. I don't believe you killed her, but I can't radiate confidence in you just to make all this seem rather ridiculous. I'm the surgeon now, Doctor, and you're the patient. Mine is

47

the authority and if I probe the wound, hurt it, then bear with me.

He nodded coolly at Mavor and told him to sit down.

"Accept my sympathy. Margaret McKendrick was your girlfriend, I believe. You were lovers?"

Ian, aware that the Inspector inteded to be brusquely direct, stiffened into hostility and then forced himself to relax. There had been a bastard like this one on one of the examining boards. Putting up resistance had almost cost him the exam.

"Yes. We went to bed together." He saw where the question was leading and forgave it. "We had a normal sexual relationship."

"So you didn't take her up to the wasteland and sexually assault her?"

"No, sir."

"During the time of the sexual assault—and the subsequent strangling—what were you doing?"

"I was in the hospital—for some of the time in the theatre—for the rest of it in the canteen."

Maybridge looked at the notes. "Your time in the theatre has been confirmed. Some members of staff saw you in the canteen, but they tend to be somewhat woolly-minded about the time you actually spent there. You had an hour and three-quarters between operations. Did you spend all that time in the canteen drinking coffee?"

"I'd earlier had a curry. It made me thirsty."

"How many cups of coffee doused the fire of your curry?"

"Three or four."

"Thirty-five minutes per cup? You seriously expect me to believe that?"

"It's not unreasonable."

No, Maybridge thought, it wasn't . . . if you were in congenial company. Mavor had sat by himself. He had bought his coffee at a coffee dispenser. He could have come and gone without anyone taking any notice of him. In a hospital this size one wouldn't particularly notice individuals unless something unusual cropped up.

"You told Detective Sergeant Stannard when he asked you if you had phoned to see if Margaret McKendrick was still at your flat that you hadn't the time." He read from the notes. "And now I'm quoting you: 'There wasn't the opportunity to phone her. I was in the operating theatre with her father until gone twelve, and then another case came in which the old man delegated to the registrar. I came off duty at five.' The old man, I take it, is Mr. McKendrick?''

"Yes. I was with him—as I said. I couldn't phone Maggie earlier in the evening. After midnight I assumed she'd gone home.''

"But after midnight you had the time?''

"Yes, but it was pointless then, I . . .''

"Not necessarily. She was probably still there.''

"I wasn't to know that.''

"If she wasn't in your flat, where was she likely to be?''

"I don't know.''

"Had she someone else—another friend—lover, perhaps?''

"No!''

"You would have been particularly angry and jealous if she had?''

"There was no one.''

It was convincingly emphatic. Maybridge decided to believe it—at least for the time-being.

"In your statement you imply that one operation followed on the heels of the other.''

"I didn't intend to make it sound that way. There was a time gap of an hour or so.''

"An hour and three-quarters.''

"Yes.''

"Which you spent in the canteen?''

"Yes . . .'' He hesitated. "Well, most of it.''

"Ah—good,'' Maybridge said pleasantly, "you're remembering. What exactly are you remembering, Doctor?''

"I went to the washroom.''

Maybridge was careful not to smile. "To relieve yourself of the fluid intake?''

"If you want to put it like that.''

"If urinate pleases you better then I'll put it more plainly. To urinate?''

"Yes, sir.''

"Then what did you do?''

"I went to my room for cigarettes.''

"Your hospital room—or your flat?"

"My room at the hospital."

"Did you smoke in your room or somewhere you could be seen?"

"In my room."

"On your own?"

"Yes."

"Pity."

"I'm sorry," Ian said stiffly, "that I can't produce an alibi."

"Well, rake around," Maybridge said. "It's extraordinary what the brain will produce under pressure." He smiled thinly. "Speaking as a layman, of course, and not a trespasser in your surgical field." He put the notes in a neat pile. "Nature abhors a vacuum—so do the police. We like to account for every minute. If you can come up with anything other than coffee and cigarettes and the washroom as time-fillers then let me know."

He changed direction suddenly and flung the question out fast. "What sort of girl was she?"

Ian felt the blood burning his cheeks. There wasn't going to be an easy answer to that. There wasn't going to be an answer at all.

Maybridge waited a moment or two but didn't repeat the question. Had his own wife been under discussion he would have reacted the same way—minus the blush. The lad was still very young.

He liked him.

He didn't believe for a moment that he had murdered her. He was sorry he had made him sweat. He summed up the situation in his mind. A couple of youngsters in love with each other. She waited around, went home late. Walked—unfortunately. It was a wonder her fond father hadn't provided her with a car. She ran into her murderer and that was it.

He told Mavor crisply that the interview was over. "We might need to see you again, of course. Or you might need to see us."

He didn't think it likely.

After he had gone he turned to Stannard. "Well?"

"I don't know, sir. Anything is possible."

"But in this case—not probable. Where was he on the night of Sally Gray's murder?"

"According to his statement, with Maggie McKendrick."

"Which she confirmed?"

"Yes."

"She meant quite a lot to him. He took the questioning pretty well."

It wasn't a particularly pleasant job they did, he thought. At the end of the day he liked to do a bit of gardening. A garden was civilised. A lot of aggro could be expended to good account in a vegetable patch. There was nothing better for unwinding than half an hour or so in a deckchair within smelling distance of his Albertine roses. He was tired, and wished right now that retirement was just around the corner instead of several years away. He asked Stannard what his anodyne was. "Golf? Fishing?"

Stannard had no anodyne and ignored the question. He pointed out that the next one on the list was Webber. "And I'd be grateful, sir, if you'd take him on your own."

"Oh? How so?"

"He's a neighbour. His wife and my wife are friends. He made a statement earlier and I handed it in. He works in medical records. You may remember?"

Maybridge didn't. "Remind me. Or have you a copy?"

Stannard had a copy. He passed it to Maybridge and Maybridge read it. Statements, he had found, tended to be either brief or circumlocutory. This—like Mavor's—was in the former category. "All right. I take your point. Send someone for him and keep out of the way until he goes."

He hesitated—nearly asked it—and then was glad he hadn't. You don't ask for character references from friends, especially when they're policemen. Friends? He looked at Stannard's departing back and wondered.

He wondered again when Webber came in.

This man had the look of an intellectual. For God's sake what kind of look was that? But he knew what he meant. Whereas Stannard was of the earth—earthy—this man seemed almost fleshless. Here you were aware of a thinking animal with a degree of sensitivity. Physically he was tall, bony, high-cheekboned, narrow-chinned. Carefully groomed.

Mavor, too, had been intelligent and perhaps even more sensitive, but his personality hadn't come over as particularly ma-

51

ture. To assume a senior role with him had been easy. He had had to be careful not to let geniality break through. With Webber there was a subtle change in the relationship and Maybridge surprised himself by standing up before indicating a chair.

Unlike Ian Mavor, George Webber was deeply aware of his surroundings and took everything in. He noticed the shorthand writer in the corner, a small, auburn-haired w.p.c. rather like Tessa. He wondered if Tessa had been interviewed yet. He had seen her in the hospital canteen during lunch but she had been with some of the other physiotherapists and they hadn't spoken. Rumour had it that when you reached this room you were looked at with some interest. He looked at Maybridge with interest and saw a benign-looking middle-aged man, short-legged and big-paunched, who was more impressive when seated. Gold-rimmed glasses, square-framed, with eyes that were disconcertingly steady. It was normal to blink—to look away. George did both and then looked back at him again.

Maybridge had the sort of antennae that picked up nervous reactions, but here he wasn't sure. Webber seemed calm. Well—why not? He probably had no reason not to be.

He began by going over the statement. "It seems that on the night of the murder you were within a hundred yards or so of where it happened."

George agreed. "So I'm told."

"And you could have been there at roughly the time of the murder."

"Together with several other people—yes."

Maybridge said mildly, "These questions have to be asked. You understand?"

"Of course."

A wasp flew in through the window and hurled itself frantically from wall to wall. The policewoman flapped at it with her notebook.

George looked back at Maybridge.

"Did you know Margaret McKendrick?"

"No. I knew of her, of course. I didn't know her." He tried to expand it; knowing it was expected of him. "Her father is a consultant here. I had heard his daughter was training in the hospital."

"Did you know her by sight?"

52

"No, I don't think so. I can't recall her."

Maybridge showed him a photograph of Maggie—a blown-up passport one—clear, not flattering, but she still looked good. He watched closely for a reaction as Webber studied it.

There was no reaction. "Her face could be familiar." He added that most of the student nurses looked the same. "There's a homogeneous quality about them. A litter of puppies. A nest of fledglings. A ward of students." He nearly included, "a whorehouse of tarts", but stopped himself. Play it sweet. "You have to look hard to discern individuals."

"Perhaps you know this one." Maybridge passed him a photograph of Sally Gray. It was taken from a studio portrait and had been carefully posed to show Sally's best features.

There was a slight reaction, but perhaps nothing more than recognition. "Yes. Nurse Gray. You'll find my statement on that in your files."

Maybridge smiled slightly. "I apologise for the overlap. Both statements should have been clipped together, of course. Her murder and that of Margaret McKendrick were identical."

"Yes. According to the newspapers."

Maybridge thought, you are being cagey. You're being very careful.

George, who knew he was, tried to relax.

Maybridge offered him a cigarette. Webber declined. Maybridge lit one himself. He had anticipated that this interview would last ten minutes. He was wrong. Thoughts of lunch receded.

"Tell me about Sally Gray."

"She was a ward sister here—but you know that. She nursed my wife after her accident." It was always painful to recall, but it had to be told. "Sue, my wife, had a fall in the garden. She had climbed a tree to retrieve our son's ball. A branch broke and she came down on her back and cracked her spine. McKendrick operated. Not successfully. She's paraplegic."

"You mean partial paralysis?" Maybridge let his natural sympathy show.

"She has very little use of her lower limbs."

"I see. I'm sorry. How did you rate Sally Gray as a nurse?"

"Competent."

"As an individual?"

"I didn't think about her on a personal level."

"Possibly not—but think about her that way now. Was she the sort to have enemies?"

"I don't know. I only knew her in her professional capacity. I couldn't come up with a character analysis in retrospect."

He had a sudden memory of Sue weeping in Sally's arms and of Sally's effort at a pep talk. "It's something you have to live with, Mrs. Webber. You'll succeed far better than you imagine. You're not the only one in this situation. Just look around you."

Looking around at the halt and the maimed, at the sick and the angry, at the brave and the resigned, hadn't done Sue much good. Looking at Sally's rounded thighs and vigorous calves as she strode purposefully up and down the ward hadn't done much good either. She might have been an angel of mercy, but her pep talks would have been more effective if she hadn't been so obviously bursting with health.

Maybridge changed course. "You mentioned your son just now. How old is he?"

"Mike is nearly five."

"Have you any other children?"

"No."

"I see."

George wondered what he saw and had a pretty shrewd idea. He stated what McKendrick said was a fact. "There could be other children. The accident hasn't ruled it out."

Our minds, Maybridge thought, run on parallel lines. You needn't have answered something I didn't ask, but it spared the embarrassment of asking it.

He changed course again. "What sort of academic qualification do you need for a job in medical records?"

"At my level—none. Just average secretarial ability."

"What sort of academic qualifications have you?"

"I read history at Oxford."

"And took a degree?"

"No."

"Why not?"

"Is it relevant?"

Maybridge's voice sharpened. "I'm not throwing questions

54

at you out of idle curiosity. People aren't divorced from their actions. Did you fail your exams or were you sent down?''

George, needled into an ill-considered response, replied with equal sharpness. "If I said sent down, you'd want to know why, and then you'd try to equate it with unstable behaviour and the murder of two girls. I didn't murder either of them. I wasn't sent down. I left because university seemed to me to be a waste of time. I had met Sue. I wanted to marry her. It would have been much more convenient for both of us if we hadn't married. But I've never regretted it and neither, I believe, has she. Does that answer you?''

No, Maybridge thought, but it goes some of the way. I'm getting to know your temperament. You're defensive. Easily annoyed. Your job bores you. You're in it because money is a boring necessity and you haven't the wit—the tenacity—or perhaps the urge to try for something better. You love your wife— you've made that plain, and it isn't a pose—and you can't accept her paralysis. Well, who could? Of all the people I've interviewed in the past two days you, Mr. Webber, interest me the most. And you interest your neighbour, too. Why else would he have asked you to write a statement before it was strictly necessary? We would have got to you in time. He needn't have hurried matters along.

He returned to the statement. "You say here that you were returning from a rehearsal. A rehearsal for what?''

"A performance of Verdi's *Otello*. I belong to the Operatic Society.''

"As a singer?''

"No. A violinist.''

"What time was the rehearsal over?''

"About eleven.''

"What did you do afterwards? I know it's in your statement. I want to hear it from you.''

"My car wasn't available so I walked home via the Downs. I sat on the Downs for a while.''

"What time would that be?''

"Getting on for twelve.''

"Did you see anyone while you were sitting there?''

"No.''

55

"You say you were on the bench overlooking the estuary—that's where Spurling Road runs near the Downs?"

"Yes."

"It's a favourite spot on a summer's night. You were on your own?"

"Yes."

"And you saw no one?"

"No."

"So no one can corroborate the time?"

"Unfortunately not." Kids having it off in a car. I'd already decided not to write anything about that. The time hadn't occurred to me.

Maybridge sensed that something was being withheld. He pressed it. "You're sure?"

"Yes."

"You walked home up Wedmore Street—a stone's throw from Buttress Way where the murder took place. You say here that there were people around—youngsters going home from a disco. You don't describe any of them. Can you describe any of them now?"

George shrugged. "Jeans—long hair—they all look the same."

"Wasn't there a single distinguishing feature that you can recall?"

"Sorry. No."

"What time would that be?"

"I'm not obsessional about time. I had been playing in an orchestra. My mind was on the music. It was probably somewhile after twelve."

"Somewhile after twelve could be any time—including the murder time. Try to give me something definite."

George said, "Well, before one—will that do?"

For the time being, Maybridge thought—but why pinpoint one? He asked, "Were you carrying your violin case?"

"Yes."

"Good. Splendid. You might not remember other people, but they, with luck, will remember you. Or if not you, your violin."

He pushed open a ballpoint pen and drew forward a fresh

56

piece of paper. "And now we'll take your statement through again—step by step—and we'll see if you can do any better."

At the end of half an hour the statement was marginally fuller, but the time gaps were still there. The walk on the Downs still seemed to have gone on for a long time. Did one sit alone in the dark, Maybridge wondered, contemplating Italian arias when one had a paralysed wife waiting at home—and a small son? He didn't ask it. This was a preliminary interview, not an interrogation in the true sense.

He stood up and thanked Webber for his co-operation. "I hope you didn't think any of the questions were offensive. They had to be asked. I hope I shan't have to bother you again."

But I will, he thought, I will.

Eight

ON THE FOLLOWING SATURDAY MIKE CELEBRATED HIS fifth birthday. Sue, with considerable help from Tessa, had made a lemon sponge cake and iced it. It was in the shape of the figure five and had candles down the middle. On his fourth birthday she had invited the neighbouring children to a party, but had vowed never to do it again. You could only cope with a lot of boisterous kids when you had your legs to stride over to the disaster areas. Her helpers, who could stride easily enough, tended not to be at the right place at the right time. George had grown angry when he should have remained calm and Tessa, who couldn't cope very well with kids, even when they were relatively civilised, had gone around looking guilty for days. The party had been her idea. "You've got to lead a normal life, Sue, as normal as you can. For Mike's sake as much as your own. Kids need parties."

This year, according to Tessa, kids needed picnics. Mike chose to ask Millicent and Royle, the seven-year-old Bray twins from next door. He was due to holiday with them in their caravan in West Bay before school started again in September, an arrangement that Sue panicked about in her less positive moments. Sylvia, their mother, was the most practical neighbour she had ever had, and the least likely to drown, lose or otherwise dispose of Mike, but homesickness when you were five and away from home for the first time in your life was something else again. Even Sylvia wouldn't be proof against that. The picnic, even if it wasn't a wild success, would at least show

how the three of them rubbed along. She suggested that Sylvia might like to join them, but Sylvia declined. "It would take the gilt off the gingerbread for Tessa. It was her idea. She wants to smother you all in her loving, motherly arms—and care for you tenderly. Sorry, Sue."

Antagonism, Sue realised surprised, runs like a subterranean river. For most of the time you don't know it's there. She understood now why Sylvia hadn't come to the party last year.

It was almost an hour's drive before the estuary opened out and the mudbanks became sand. They were aiming for Cormorant Cove, a small beach Sue had played on when she was a child, but had forgotten, until they reached there, how awkward it was to get to. Tessa had driven ahead with the children and her car was already parked on the headland.

George drove up beside it and got out. He could hear Tessa calling to the children as they hurled themselves down the cliff path. She was half-slipping, half-running after them, and then she tripped and rolled the last few yards into a sand dune. Mike, screaming with laughter, came and sat on her stomach. She shook the sand out of her hair and hugged him and laughed and forgot about Sue somewhere up at the top.

George, looking down at her, felt a burst of exasperation. God almighty, couldn't she see the place was impossible? He returned to Sue and suggested that they should drive on to the main beach half a mile away.

Sue wouldn't agree. "It will be easier to carry me down than to get Tessa to persuade everyone up again."

"I'll round them up. Just give me five minutes."

But she wanted to go down. This place was a memory place. She wanted to see her child enjoying it.

The wheelchair was a folding one and was in the boot. It couldn't be used here. George took out the wicker picnic basket and went down first with that.

Tessa went to meet him. "We're staying? I thought Sue might want to go on."

"She doesn't. It would be far more sensible if she did." He found a patch of shade and put the basket in it. "Do you think you can sit on that and stop the kids getting into it?"

He was wearing shorts and a navy towelling shirt. The wind was roughing up his hair. She had never seen him looking carefree but he almost looked it now. He smiled at her. "It was lucky you had a soft landing. Any damage?"

"No. I'm okay. Fine."

She watched him as he went up again. He was thin and wiry and strong enough to hoist Sue over his shoulder and start the careful descent. Even at a distance Tessa sensed his tenderness as he held her. Her dark hair was falling over her face. Her limbs looked slim and normal and had already tanned a pale coffee colour after hours of sitting in the garden with a book. Their minds matched. They were both readers. She had once or twice fetched Sue books from the library but had guessed they hadn't been read. George fetched them now together with his own about twice a week. "Even if I could move," Sue had confessed to her once, "I'd make a rotten housewife. It's as well housework bores me."

Tessa had said in mitigation for her shining home that she had thought Brecht's *Threepenny Opera* was a book for children.

Sue, knowing she wasn't joking, had laughed with a sudden warm surge of affection. "You're kind to me, Tessa. Have I ever said that to you before?"

She hadn't.

Kind?

Motivation?

Pure honest to God willingness to help?

They had reached the bottom now and the children were running up to them. Mike took a fistful of his mother's hair and put it across his lips like a moustache. George told him to scarper and find a place where his mother could sit. The children cleared an area of stones and seaweed and Royle turned round and round on his bottom and then stood up and, indicating the hollow, said, "Here, Auntie Sue, sit here."

Sue thanked him gravely from her upside-down position and George lowered her gently into it. Millicent primly straightened her yellow cotton skirt. "You were showing your panties, Auntie Sue."

Sue, amused, reached over for George's hand and squeezed it. She was glad she'd come. The beach was beautiful. It was also empty. She hadn't yet learnt to live with the stares of strangers. Her small stock of four-letter words mumbled *sotto voce* was the only defence mechanism she had. Here her vocabulary could be pure. Here she could sit and do absolutely nothing and not care. The children were to be observed but not worried about. George and Tessa would cope. It would be very much nicer if George could cope without Tessa, but one had to be a realist. That he, too, would like to be able to cope without Tessa was something she knew. It was his nature to keep the outside world outside.

Or, at times, to walk alone in it.

A seagull swooped inland and dropped a mouldy piece of bread near her feet. A cloud momentarily obliterated the sun. She shivered and closed her eyes. When she opened them again the sun was creeping over the sand like a wash of deep yellow and someone had heeled in the bread.

Your imagination, she told herself, is as maimed as your legs. So he sometimes comes in late—so what? He doesn't have to come in at all. He cossets you, puts up with you—loves you. If he's got a whore who gives him what you can't then so be it. *And stop thinking about it.*

He had told her about the interview with Maybridge. "If the police ask you what time I got in then say twelve-thirty—it's near enough."

They had avoided looking at each other and she hadn't said anything more than a subdued, "Yes".

Put it out of your mind.

The cliffs were a windbreak and it was warm enough to bathe. Tessa and George went in with the children and Sue sat and trickled the sand over her legs and watched them. It looked like a family scene in which she played the role of grandmother looking on with indulgent amusement. Only amusement wasn't the word. Neither was resentment at this particular moment. Both George and Tessa were good swimmers, but they didn't swim too far from the children. Royle was teaching Mike the breast-stroke, or trying to. Millicent, like a fat little pòrpoise, was floating and singing to herself. The two-year age gap between the twins and Mike didn't seem to matter. All three were getting on together very well. The holiday might work. She tried to imagine Mike at seven. He would be going to the junior school. He had lost out on attention in the last couple of years. At times she tried to make up for it and over-compensated. She hoped he would grow up blessedly free of anxiety and the trap of total commitment. He wasn't like George in temperament, though very much like him in looks. When you're grown, she told him in her mind, find out what you'd like to do and whatever it is do it. Don't be deflected. And if and when you marry—and take your time about that—don't marry a girl who's accident-prone. I love you sweetie, and I love your dad.

For Tessa it was a day without a flaw. There was wind and sun and sandy birthday cake. Cold, wet bodies of children— rough towels—salty lips. George's laughter—rare, but filling her with delight. When he played with the children he became warm and approachable. They clung around his neck and he rolled them in the sand.

She sat a little away from Sue, her back against a rock, and watched him. She imagined that the three children were hers and that he was the father. They were all living in Connemara—on a farm. And then she changed her mind about the farm. It didn't suit him. Louis suited the farm—the more mundane side of it where chickens had their necks wrung and pigs were killed. George in a fisherman's cottage in Galway— out with the trawlers in the daytime, back home with his books at night. A peat fire. The built-up bed in the little room adjoining the living room—a bed with wooden sides like a ship's bunk—a feather mattress, squashy and warm—George beneath her—George sideways to her—George in all the ways that Louis demanded and she refused—George totally and wholly and in any way he wanted loving her—flesh of her flesh. She closed her eyes and dreamed on.

At five o'clock it clouded over and began to get cold. Mike threw sand into Royle's ear and George cleaned it out with a handkerchief dipped in a rock pool. It was time to go home.

It was more difficult carrying Sue back up the path and George started to get winded, but tried not to make it obvious. When he put her down at the top she pulled his face down to hers and kissed him. "Don't dare get a heart attack on my account."

Tessa, still dream-wrapped, saw and didn't care. His tenderness to Sue was part of his image. He was a *good* man. He reminded her of Father Leary. She had fantasied about him when she was twelve—but within strict Catholic limits. His eyes had been like the sea at twilight. Her thoughts hadn't travelled over his anatomy in any other direction.

When she got home she saw that Louis had been and gone. There was a note propped up on the fridge. "Don't you ever fill this thing? I've gone out for a meal."

He came back at ten smelling of beer and fish and chips. She looked pointedly at his unshaven chin.

He said tiredly, "I needed food. I need sleep. It would be too inconvenient, I suppose, to say I need you?"

She told him, without having to lie about it, that she had the curse.

He thought she looked magnificent. Sunburnt. Exuding warmth, though not for him. Untidy. Almost wanton. He asked her where she'd been. She told him.

"So you and George had a lovely day." It was mocking.

"And Sue and the children."

"Oh yes," he said. "And Sue and the children . . . children?"

"The Bray twins across the road."

George and Sue and several kids, he thought. Very respectable. Very proper. He had been about to make a joke about it, but stopped himself. His sort of jokes weren't her sort of jokes. Not that there was anything funny about any of it. Bitter, vulgar, bar humour was a defensive weapon he wielded clumsily. He knew there were times when he disgusted her. There were times, too, when he deliberately hurt her. If you didn't care about a person you were meticulously polite. You didn't get within touching distance. With Tessa he had to force his way through to her. He wished he could just turn his back on her, and not care.

Nine

Six weeks after the murder of Sally Gray, Rachel nearly knifed Police Constable Bill Crawley to death. It happened in the Cathedral graveyard at twenty minutes to midnight. He had been assigned the job of tailing her and wasn't very good at it. He had come to the conclusion that he wasn't very good at police work at all, and wanted out.

Being a detective constable was marginally better than being in the uniformed branch, but only insofar as he could frequent the the local pubs without being too obvious. He had been out of uniform now for over twelve months and had been drinking on duty and getting away with it for some time. On this Wednesday night he had settled himself at The Feathers and waited in the warmth until it was her time to go by. On her off-duty nights she took the walk her sister had taken and hardly ever varied the route. Bored, he plodded along behind her. Not too close, but not too well concealed either. It was a wet night and the cypress trees dripped water like mourners' tears. His grandmother had been buried over on the west side of the cemetery six months ago. He had been fond of her and thought he might break the routine a little by going in search of the grave. Rachel, also breaking the routine by taking a different direction, met him head-on. He lost his footing and stumbled on top of her.

Shaking with fright, she tried a judo throw that didn't work—he just rolled away mildly astonished. Sobbing, she pulled out the paper knife and aimed it at his chest. It splintered

64

his mac button and would have done further harm if he hadn't twisted her wrist and taken it from her. She opened her mouth to scream and he clamped his hand over her face and stopped her. Thinking he was going for her throat she fainted for the first time in her life.

When she came to she was sitting on the grass with her head pushed down between her knees and her assailant, as upset as she was, was telling her to calm down. He was aggrieved. "You bloody nearly killed me." He told her he was there for her protection. "I've been following you on your idiotic walks for days." He helped her to sit up.

She began to cry. It was good to be alive. She didn't know whether she believed him or not, but at least she was temporarily alive. He sensed her doubt and showed her his police identity card which she couldn't see in the dark, so he shone his torch on it. And then he shone his torch on his splintered button and said "Christ!"

She began to laugh and her tears took a wrong direction down her windpipe so that she choked and gasped. Finally, she was sick. He turned his head away, disgusted. When she was better he proffered his handkerchief. She declined it. She had her own.

"You know," he said at last, "that I shall have to report that you had an offensive weapon—and that you tried to use it?"

She said meekly that she was sorry and could she have it back, please.

"Certainly not."

She suggested that they might sit in the Cathedral porch out of the rain and discuss the matter further. He reminded her of the young mathematics teacher who had tried to teach her O-level algebra. He, too, had confiscated things and had once almost wept when the more unruly elements had pelted him with chalk. Here was a man with a soft core. And thank God for that. She too wondered why he had chosen the police force.

He declined to sit in the porch, pointing out reasonably that it was much too cold.

"Then what are you going to do?"

"Take you back to the police station and make a report."

"Tell them that I blew your cover, you mean? Tell them that you were so good at tailing me that you fell on top of me?"

He tried to brush some of the mud off his mac. She had a point. If he left the police force, and he had almost decided to leave, then he would need a decent reference. His performance tonight wouldn't elicit paeans of praise.

He decided to compromise. "If I get rid of your knife will you promise me you won't get another one?"

Infant child! she thought, astonished at his naïvety, and then she got a whiff of his breath and realised just how much he had been drinking. Another thought followed on the heels of the first—if he had been the murderer the knife would have been about as effective as a baby's rattle. So who was naïve?

"All right," she said. "I promise."

She watched with amusement as he walked off into the darkness. It took him five minutes to find his grandmother's grave and he buried it at her feet where the mud was soft under the chippings. "Amen", he said to it—and to her. Everything had an end—even this bloody job.

When he returned to Rachel he told her that he wouldn't be tailing her again.

That was too obvious for comment. She asked him if anyone else would.

"If I tell them about tonight—yes."

"But you won't?"

His conscience put up a feeble flutter. "Someone has to protect you. If you keep on looking for someone to do you in, you'll find him."

She said sarcastically, "It's awfully nice of you to care." And then, because she was still shaken, she apologised. She knew that she could never take this walk alone in the darkness again. She was supremely grateful that the police cared enough about her safety to send someone—even this overgrown schoolboy—to keep an eye on her. It occurred to her that if he returned to base in his present condition he was quite likely to get the sack.

She suggested that he might like to go and have a few cups of strong black coffee in the coffee bar on the other side of the square. "And if they have a peppermint dispenser, then get some."

He asked her with an attempt at dignity if she thought he had been drinking. She answered with extreme tact that coffee was warming on a cold night and that the mints were good to chew.

He wasn't fooled and was grateful.

It was out of gratitude that he told her what he shouldn't. "The sort of person who did your sister in," he said, "and Maggie McKendrick—and you, if you don't stop these stupid walks—is a nutter with a hang-up about sex. The Chief Inspector has started a shortlist. I can't remember any of the names on it—but one of them does amateur dramatics—or sings—or plays the fiddle—or watches ballet, or somesuch nonsense. Did your sister ever dance?"

Rachel, very quiet and cold, said No—Sally never danced. "But tell me more."

He was sober enough to know he had told her too much. "I don't know any more. Go home now—and take care."

She laid a restraining hand on his arm. "Give me names—think!"

Disturbed by his indiscretion he began to lose his temper. "What are you trying to do—corrupt me?"

"If that's a hint you'll tell me for money, then tell me how much?"

Deeply affronted he turned and left her.

She called after him through the rain that she was sorry. Sorry, she thought, sorry, sorry. I handled you badly. I should have brought you home. Tanked you up with more booze. Oh hell—oh, bloody, bloody hell.

Eventually, when calmer, she realised that the night wasn't the disaster it had seemed.

She was alive.

The police had a shortlist.

Someone in the art world—wide as that might be—was on it.

It was a beginning.

Ten

PAUL HAD BOUGHT TWO TICKETS FOR THE OPERA, ONE FOR himself and one for Maggie, well ahead of the day of the performance. The local operatic society, though not of professional quality, was nevertheless good. Seeing the tickets on his desk in his study was one of the many painful reminders of a situation he knew he could never accept. He was about to tear them up but changed his mind. Harriet was an ardent fan of Verdi and he had overheard her saying she had failed to get tickets. He took them down to the hospital with him.

At first she said, no, she didn't want to go, and then tried to persuade him to go with her. For him grief went a lot deeper than the conventional behaviour of the bereaved. Maggie was too recently dead for him to appear at a public function, but that didn't bother him. Maggie, in the normal way, would have been there sitting beside him, and that he couldn't take. At the risk of underlining Harriet's insensitivity by spelling it out, he spelled it out.

She understood belatedly and though mildly hurt accepted it. She would go, she said, and take anyone along who would like the spare ticket.

Despite the difference in age and professional seniority she invited Ian Mavor.

They were scrubbing up together when she suggested it. "Or will you be on call?"

He hesitated. He wasn't on call. He wished he were so that he could opt out politely. Since Maggie's murder he had had no social life. Instead he had directed all his energy into studying for Primary Fellowship.

Harriet said gently, "A night out would do you good—preferably with someone your own age. I don't mind relinquishing my ticket if there's someone else you'd rather go with."

There wasn't anyone else. He didn't think there ever would be. And put like that he couldn't refuse.

Paul heard of the arrangement with a degree of surprise. Under the circumstances it was extremely unlikely that Mavor had accepted with any enthusiasm. Paul had begun to take an interest in him; and not just on Maggie's account. He was a promising surgeon. Paul was giving a lecture that afternoon on tumours of the peripheral nerves and afterwards he took Ian aside to follow up a discussion on axon degeneration.

"I see you're not a compulsive note-taker. May I?"

Ian handed him his notebook.

Paul studied it. Every point had been covered. "You work as I used to work. I like your diagrams. Examiners don't like wading through waffle. If there's anything you want to discuss at any time don't hesitate to come to me."

"Thank you, sir."

Maggie. I want to discuss Maggie. Your daughter during all the years I didn't know her. I want to see old snaps of her. On holiday. In school. In France. Here. The home she shared with you. Her bedroom. The bed. Does the sun shine on it in the morning? Did she wake up to sun? The bathroom. The smell of her soap. She had a dog. I've never seen it. I want to hear her dog bark. I had her for three months. Intimately. Every soft crevice of her flesh. But I want more. Maggie whole. Put together by all the memories you have and I haven't.

I want to blot out that last night.

I want to cut it out like a carcinoma and begin to heal.

Tell me about her.

Paul, collecting up his papers, looked at him thoughtfully. He sensed an unexpressed need and didn't understand. He could speak freely enough about his work, but that was as far as communication between them went. Were all young people so inarticulate? Was it rank that was bothering him?

"By the nature of the job," he told him, "we surgeons are

69

removed to some extent from too close an emotional contact with our patients. For most of the time they're interesting organs on the operating table. Inevitably, though, we do have to meet them from time to time as people—usually frightened people. It's an aspect of the job that can't be taught. Do you find that side of things difficult?''

"To recognise pain," Ian said, "you have to know pain. Let's say I'm learning."

Paul looked away from him. "There's no more news. The Chief Constable is in touch with me. As soon as I hear anything I'll let you know."

"Has he told you anything at all?"

"Only that they have a list of names. Three have a history of psychosexual disorders. Four have been inside, but are otherwise normal—if you can define normality. Some others, I can't remember the number, have no criminal record and no record of psychiatric disturbance, but for reasons best known to the police they're listed. Until someone is charged the police guard the list like Fort Knox."

"And if they go through them one by one," Ian said, "and they're all in the clear—what then?"

It was the second time he had raised the question. Paul remembered the first time. The boy was becoming obsessional. But he wasn't alone in that.

He grimaced. "There's a phrase about assisting the police in their enquiries—a literal application might be in order. Let's hope it won't come to that."

Shouting in the dark, he thought, as he went back to his consulting room. If the police fail, how can I or anyone else succeed? He had done all he could to prise names out of the Chief Constable but Rendcome had been adamant. "The only name I'll mention to you is one you've already mentioned to me. Your Owen something or something Owen is Owen Llewellyn. As you've already told me, he was one of Maggie's friends. As you haven't told me, and perhaps don't know, he was born in North Wales. The family has since moved to Liverpool. His father is a retired school teacher. His mother died two years ago. As you've already told me, he is an economics student. You haven't told me he's a Marxist. You probably don't know—and it doesn't make a ha'porth of difference anyway. My reason for telling you all this is to demonstrate that we come up with every last detail of anyone who had any connection with Maggie whatsoever. We're thorough. We're also discreet. Llewellyn is not on the list. If he had been I would have appeared to have forgotten that you ever mentioned him. I don't walk into your operating theatre, Paul, and demand a scalpel. I let you get on with it.''

And so, get on with it, Paul thought, as he drew out his appointment book, and keep on getting on with it. But get him.

He spoke to his secretary on the intercom, ''I see one of the hospital staff wants an interview about his wife. Which department is he in?''

''Medical records, Mr. McKendrick.''

''I could slot him in for ten minutes now if he can manage to get over. Have you his wife's notes?''

She had, of course. Mary Timms was one of the most efficient secretaries he had ever had . . . and the youngest. She was twenty-one and looked eighteen. She brought them in and put them on his desk.

He began to read the notes but realised she had something else to say. ''Yes—Mary, what is it?''

''You have a new theatre sister, Mr. McKendrick, starting next week.''

He already knew that and said ''Yes?'' impatiently.

Mary coloured up as if he'd slapped her. ''Well, I don't suppose it matters, but I thought you ought to know—if you don't know already.''

He was instantly reminded of Rendcome's speech. It was circumlocutory, but the point, when he came to it, had been valid. ''Know what?''

Mary's point was valid, too. ''She's Rachel Gray. Sally Gray's sister.''

''Oh.'' He hadn't known. It was an appointment singularly lacking in tact. Tact? Odd word to spring to mind. Presumably if she didn't mind the association, then why should he? He wondered why she had applied for the job in the first place. Obviously she had the right qualifications and obviously applicants weren't thick on the ground. He could veto the appointment now, he supposed, but why? What arguments were there against it? When I look at her I'll see Maggie—and when she looks at me. . . ? Sally Gray. If she were anything like her sister she would be efficient, dependable, a good nurse. If they could both blank their minds to the . . . murders . . . a malignant word, difficult to form, like a carcinoma in the throat—then the association could work.

Mary was waiting for him to voice his reaction, her cheeks still flushed.

He told her quite gently that he hadn't known, but was glad that she had told him. He added, "It makes no difference."

"Well, that's all right, then."

"Yes."

"I'll send Mr. Webber in as soon as he arrives—or do you need more time with the notes?"

"No, send him in."

A quick glance had told him everything he needed to know. He remembered Sue Webber quite clearly. The injuries had been severe. Apart from relieving compression by removing fragments of bone from the fractured vertebrae which had penetrated the spinal cord there was nothing he could do. There had been absolutely no way of preventing the paralysis. In some operations where there was a slight possibility of success, and one failed, one needed to anaesthetise one's sense of self-criticism in order to survive in the job. In this case his conscience was clear. He couldn't have done more. No one could. He remembered Webber's reaction when he told him that his wife wouldn't walk again. He hadn't spoken. He had stood in the centre of the consulting room, his hands clenched at his sides, and the sweat had broken out on his face and neck so that he seemed to have been washed in oil.

Having so recently discussed this sort of situation with Ian with what must have seemed godlike condescension it was ironical to be faced with it now.

He stood up as George Webber was shown in and indicated a chair. The last two years should have smoothed out some of the tensions, but he saw that they hadn't. He was about a stone underweight.

"You've come to talk to me about Sue?"

The personal approach, George thought. Sue. Your wife—or even Mrs. Webber—would have put the interview on a slightly different level. Pals together. Colleagues. Sue.

Paul sensed the antagonism. He understood it and didn't blame him, but if he had to defend his professional skill he would defend it. He sat back, waiting.

George said, "Yes, I've come to talk about Sue. I don't know how much time you've got—or how irrelevant this might seem—but a short while ago our son was five. We took him on a birthday picnic, together with two other children and a friend—a girl as near my wife's age as makes no difference. May I tell you about it?"

Paul pushed forward his cigarette box. "Carry on."

George took a cigarette and lit it. "It was a pleasant day—the sun shone. The children and the other girl ran down to the beach. I carried my wife down—slung across my shoulder. The children and the other girl and I went into the sea. We used our limbs—swam. Sue sat on the beach—in the spot where she had been put—and couldn't move away from. She smiled. Waved. And sat. When we were first married she was a better swimmer than I was. She could move in the water like an eel. After the children came out they had to be dressed. My son teased her by putting his sandal out of her reach. I could have slapped him. She laughed. She's good at laughing. But not all the time. There were candles on the birthday cake. The other girl lit them. There was a breeze and she had to kneel up to do it and turn her body this way and that to stop the lighter going out. Sue watched. She's good at watching. After tea the children and the other girl played ball. Sue told me to join them. I did, to please her. We got very warm. When I returned to Sue I put my hand on hers. It was cold. Her cardigan was out of her reach. I put it around her. The children and the other girl glowed like candles on a Christmas tree. They had one hell of a good day. Sue had, too. Within her limits. I'm finding those limits increasingly hard to take. I want to know what can be done about it."

Paul said, "Wait a minute." He buzzed for Mary and when she came told her to send in coffee. "And don't put any calls through unless they're urgent."

When she had gone he took out a sheet of paper and a couple of coloured pens.

"Before we discuss this any further, I think you should be put wise to the type of injury she sustained, and the nature of the operation. Pull your chair up to the desk and I'll make it as

73

clear as I can." He drew a thick line down the centre of the paper. "This is the spinal cord—the area of the lesion was here." He marked it. "These are the nerves involved. Have you any knowledge of anatomy at all?"

George moved impatiently and ash from his cigarette fell on to the diagram. "I have no medical knowledge, but I can draw what you've drawn with my eyes shut. I've read every medical book I could lay my hands on. I've had a second and third opinion from other men in your field. They upheld you. They praised your skill. All right, I didn't expect anything different. You would uphold them. They say another operation would do no good. Perhaps that's the ethical thing to say. But you've been inside her. You know. Can you operate on her again? Can you make her better?"

Anger was pointless and pity didn't help. Paul experienced both briefly and then retired behind a screen of professional calm. "No—I'm sorry. If a second operation would have done any good I would have told you. The quality of Sue's life depends on her personality—and on you. Other girls in her position have used their talents within their physical limits. As I remember her, she is intelligent. You say your lad is five. Of school age. Her days are free. She could use them studying— for a degree, even. There's the Open University, has she thought of that? Her legs are paralysed, not her brain. The world is outside waiting for her. If she has the guts to make the effort she can go out into it. There'll be willing helpers. It's up to her to accept her condition—and for you to accept her condition."

George pushed back his chair and stood up. "I've heard all that before. It's called a positive approach. Open University? She has a degree already. She's qualified to teach. Can you imagine Sue in her wheelchair in a modern comprehensive? Oh yes, it's been done. Others have done it. She didn't like teaching when she had her two legs to get around on. Guts? She's not timid and she'll put up a fight if she has to—but why should she? She likes to read—and thank God for that—but if she went to the library to choose her own books she'd have to cross two main roads in her wheelchair and no zebra crossing. And when and if she got there, how would she get up the steps? That's what we're talking about—mundane, ordinary things like roads

74

with traffic on them—and steps—and not having enough room to make a downstairs lavatory. And don't tell me about appliances—and social services—and brilliantly coping paraplegics who can do this and that and put everyone else to shame. Sue is ordinary. Sometimes she tries very hard. Sometimes she doesn't. She was making a jersey for Mike once and the wool fell under the sideboard. When she tried to get it out it got twisted around one of the supports. What did she do? Shrug and go back to her book? Wheel herself into the kitchen and make a cake? On another day she might have. Not that day. She took out the cutlery and flung it as hard as she could in every direction. She didn't cry until I got home and began picking it up again. I love her. If there was any part of my body that I could give her to make her whole, I would give it. I've put off coming to see you; I knew what you'd say. I've gone over this conversation in my mind many times. Sue doesn't know I'm here and I shan't tell her I've been. She keeps thinking she can will herself well. That she'll wake up one day and, hey presto, she'll be able to do what all the other women can do . . . like getting out of bed by herself . . . getting to Mike in a hurry when he falls . . . coming to me . . . to my bed, when she . . .''

The torrent of words stopped momentarily as he strove to be calm. ''And that's something else again. We haven't had sexual intercourse since the operation. Her sexual feelings are as dead as her legs. I know what you said about her being able to bear a child despite the paralysis. You didn't say the sex act would fill her with revulsion. There was a lot you didn't say—didn't admit to—didn't know. I love her . . . I want her . . . I want her as she used to be before you got your goddamn healing hands on her.''

His voice was thickening and he couldn't clearly see where he was going as he made for the door. He had to get out before he broke down in front of the incompetent bastard behind the desk. He didn't deliberately knock the tray of coffee out of Mary's hands as she came in with it. The hot liquid didn't touch her, but it splashed the carpet and the walls.

Paul whispered, ''Jesus!'' He went over to Mary to reassure her and to help mop up the mess. He had rarely had condemna-

tory confrontations with patients' relatives before, and never
one as viciously personal or as bitter as this.

Eleven

THE SET-TO IN THE CHURCHYARD HADN'T DONE RACHEL'S shoulder much good. Theatre work wouldn't involve any heavy lifting, but it was always better to start a new appointment whole. She had applied for the job on impulse. One prodded an aching tooth, but if one had any sense one left it alone. She was fast discovering that good sense wasn't one of her assets. There could be no camaraderie with McKendrick, the association would be professional, nothing more; but she wanted to be near someone who felt what she felt. Hate was like a battery on charge—a double charge might produce better results. From now on the night walk alone was out, but the intention behind it remained the same. The police might sit around on their asses, but she would never give up. If McKendrick were of similar calibre then neither would he.

She went into the physiotherapy department to see if Tessa could give her extra treatment. The room reminded her of a toy department full of mechanised dolls. Pull this—move that—lift the zimmer—forward—down—one, two, well done—pummel—breathe—push—try, dear, try.

Tessa, giving an arthritic patient wax therapy on his hands, was droning away placidly, "No, you won't find it uncomfortable—just very soothing. Now, doesn't that feel marvelous? No—let them stay. Just like that. Cure you? Well, no, love—it will just ease your joints a little."

Rachel went and stood beside her and told her she had pulled the muscle in her shoulder again. "I slipped in the bedroom."

The patient made sympathetic noises. Tessa, less than sympathetic, said that her list for that afternoon was full.

"Could you slot me in at the end of the day? Then afterwards we might have that drink we arranged?"

Tessa compromised. "I can give you twenty minutes' heat treatment, but I'm meeting someone at four-thirty."

When Rachel returned at four Tessa took her into a cubicle at the end of the room and turned on the lamp. Because she didn't like Rachel and never intended at any time having another drink with her she became voluble in her excuses and talked too much. "I'm going to buy a dress for a friend of mine. She used to be a patient here. She's paraplegic. Her husband works in medical records. He plays the violin in the operatic society. He thinks if he gives his wife a new dress she might be persuaded to go to the performance. Verdi's *Otello*. He's been rehearsing for it for weeks. It should be very good. Are you going?"

Rachel said no, she wasn't going. She felt hot, lazy and bored. The little Irish physio fizzed conversationally like a bottle of lemonade. And then, suddenly, she was bored no more. She sat up and nearly knocked the lamp over.

Tessa pulled it back. "Sorry—were you getting too hot?"

"No. Yes." She lay down again and carefully levelling all interest out of her voice asked who the paralysed patient was.

Tessa told her. She added. "They live across the road from us. He's a marvellous husband, absolutely devoted to her."

A fiddle player, the policeman had said, a singer, or a watcher of ballet, or some such nonsense. Someone with a sexual hang-up . . . like the husband of a paralysed wife?

Her heart was thumping and she felt sick. She wiped the back of her hand across her forehead.

Tessa, surprised, turned off the lamp. "You've had enough. You didn't react like this last time."

"I don't feel well. I'm sorry. If I could have a drink of water. . . ?"

Tessa fetched it and watched her with some concern as she drank it. "If I hadn't promised to meet George I'd drive you home." It was the least she could say.

"George? Oh, the husband is going shopping with you?"

"Yes." Tessa's pleasure at the prospect glowed out of her like sunlight.

Rachel watched her over the rim of her glass. So that was the way of it. This association was worth cultivating. It was a pity the girl was so hostile to her.

"Did Sally know the Webbers?"

"Well, naturally, Sue was her patient."

"She never mentioned them. Obviously she didn't know them as well as you know them."(Until, perhaps, the end?)

"Sally wasn't a neighbour of theirs."

"Well no, obviously not. If she had been, I would have been. We lived together—remember?"

Tessa, instinctively aware that the conversation should be closed, said she had to go. "Rest your arm and stop falling around. It's as well you're taking time off nursing these days— that's the best of agency nursing, I should think—the freedom."

"Which ends on Monday." Rachel explained that she was joining the permanent staff.

Tessa received the news without enthusiasm.

The Webbers were on the phone and the telephone book gave their address. Rachel called the following evening hoping to find both of them in, but it was Sue who opened the door. The latch had been lowered so that she could reach it from her wheelchair. She sat looking up enquiringly at Rachel, and Rachel, momentarily disconcerted, looked down at her. She saw a slim woman in a red blouse and navy denims. Her hair, worn loose, swept over the back of the chair like a black waterfall.

Rachel's rehearsed sentences came out smoothly. "I'm awfully sorry to bother you, but I've been trying to get tickets for the opera and it seems the only hope is that members of the cast might not have used all of their allocation. Your friend Tessa told me that Mr. Webber plays in the orchestra." She added, unnecessarily as she was wearing her uniform, that she was a nurse. "A colleague of Tessa's. I didn't know where else to try."

Sue accepted her at face value and invited her in. "My husband's out with Mike—our son. They probably won't be very long. You can wait for a while, if you have the time."

("You're vulnerable in your wheelchair," George had told her once. "Don't ask strangers in." "For God's sake, why?"

79

she had retorted irritably. "Nobody's going to cosh me and make off with the non-existent silver.")

She smiled at her primly spoken guest, but despite the reassuringly familiar uniform felt a slight twinge of unease. It had all come out very pat. And what was that about allocation of tickets? As far as she knew George had three—one each and one for Tessa.

Rachel looked around the room curiously. Lots of books. Pieces of Leggo on the bureau. The child's pyjamas airing on the radiator. A small modern piano with a scratched lid piled high with sheet music. Bottles of Scotch, gin and sherry on a trolley behind the door. Ash trays with ash and stubbed cigarette ends in them. Finally her eyes turned to Sue. Somehow she gave the place dignity, sitting there in her wheelchair in the middle of the grotty room, apparently not giving a damn about the grot. I like you, she thought. But you're as wary as hell of me, and I wish you weren't.

She smiled and her smile was honest.

Sue responded to it and relaxed. "Cigarette?"

"Thanks, but I don't." (A small Scotch would be acceptable.)

Sue picked up the suggestion but ignored it. The monthly budget didn't run to drinks. She wished the bottles of booze could be kept tactfully out of sight where they wouldn't bleed the bank balance even redder. She decided she would offer tea later if George were late. What sort of conversation did you strike up with a stranger? The weather? Chilly for August, isn't it? Nursing? How long have you been at the City Hospital?

"How long have you been at the City Hospital?"

Rachel sat back on the lumpy sofa and crossed her legs. "I'm an agency nurse. I start at the City Hospital on Monday. When you do agency nursing you get around." She began inventing. "I've just been to see a private patient, ten minutes from here. That's why I called here this evening, more or less on the spur of the moment. I hope you don't mind?"

Sue said she didn't mind. "But I think it's quite unlikely that George has any extra tickets. If he has they'll be in the bureau."

She wheeled her chair over to it and opened the lid. As well as paper and envelopes there was an assortment of old snapshots, boxes of crayons, half a bar of chocolate, an old clock key, four rubbers, one of Mike's socks (how did that get there? She took it out and put it in the pocket of her denims), a dictionary, a ruler, an out-of-date guarantee for the television tube, and finally an envelope with 'Milk—four pints please', written on it. The tickets were inside. Just three. She took them out and showed them to Rachel.

"I'm sorry. Had there been any more I'm pretty sure they would have all been in together."

And now you'll go, she thought hopefully.

Rachel thanked her for looking. "You manage your chair very well."

"I'd manage better if the room were larger. The hall had to be widened to let the chair through from the front door to the kitchen. It's the same upstairs—wide corridor—small bedrooms."

"Just before Christmas," Rachel said, inventing again, "I'm booked to nurse a paraplegic."

"Really—? Nursed any Hottentots recently?" Sue's spark of anger disappeared as swiftly as it had come and they both grinned at each other in embarrassment.

Rachel said, "Sorry—but I get your point."

"Most people don't. Your lot—your well-intentioned lot— have got me near screaming more than once. Do you know about occupational therapy? Well, you do, of course. 'Mrs. Webber, how would you like to learn to tat—to make things with copper—to paint? Well, dear—there's always knitting.' Oh, they mean well, and I'm boorish to criticise. But I'm me— damn it! How old is your . . . paraplegic?"

Rachel, stressing the word, said that her patient was about the same age as Sue—thirtyish.

"Male or female?"

"Female."

"Married or single?"

"Married."

"Children?"

"A daughter of seven."

It was near enough. She was dealing with a sharp mind. She felt on the edge of discovery and was uncomfortable.

Sue's sense of unease was slowly coming back. "Like me—in fact?"

"In a way—yes."

Is that why you came—the tickets were just a blind? She didn't ask it, but it was plain that she thought it.

Rachel, aware that she had precipitated her exit, stood up reluctantly. "I didn't mean to pry—I probably shouldn't have mentioned it. Thanks for looking for the tickets."

"Wait a minute." Sue wheeled herself over to the fireplace and took down a photograph from the mantelshelf. "That was the three of us two years ago before the accident."

Rachel took the photograph and examined it. It was the man she paid particular attention to. She had watched him leaving the hospital with Tessa and his face had been indelibly printed on her brain. The face of a killer? Perhaps. A tall, thin, ill-looking man at whom Tessa was prattling. His impatience, politely held in check as he listened, had been obvious. The man in the photograph looked a great deal younger. He had his arm around his wife's shoulder and she was standing up. The child, very like him, was holding his mother's hand.

"Paraplegia," Sue said, "is more traumatic than you'll ever know. I keep wanting to get back to that, but I'm pointed in the direction of the future and told to get on with it. I react my way. Your patient will react her way. There's no common denominator—apart from the fact that our legs don't function. I have my high moments when the sun shines—there's something good on the telly—I read a book that's worth reading—Mike gets the chuckles over something daft—well, you know . . . or if you don't you can imagine . . ."

And your husband, Rachel thought, tell me about your husband. But on that Sue was silent. "There are," she said, "low moments, too. And not just for your patient, but for the whole family. Unless your patient is a wonder woman—or a saint—she'll drive you off your rocker from time to time. You have my sympathy, believe me. I hope you can stand it."

Twelve

It was in a low moment that George gave Sue the dress. It was badly mistimed. Mike, though looking forward very much to going on holiday with the Bray twins, declared that he wouldn't wear his rubber pants in the caravan bed. "But darling," Sue expostulated, "you've agreed to wear them in your bed here. You've worn them for the past week."

"My bed here's different. It's private."

"The bed there is private, too. It's a bunk and you're having it to yourself."

"I'll get up and go to the lavatory."

"That's what you say you'll do here, but you pee in your sleep."

"Then I won't sleep."

"It might be better," George interposed, "if you don't go."

Sue, until that moment ambivalent, became quite sure that he should go. "He'll have a natural, carefree holiday with them. It will compensate for all this." In a gesture of despair she indicated the wheelchair and the general chaos.

George, tired and edgy, began picking up Mike's toys and an assortment of what Sue called domestic trivia. He didn't know why a dishcloth should find its way into the living room, but it had and he took it back to the kitchen.

Sue ordered Mike to clear away his toys himself. "Your father spoils you. The twins' father won't spoil you. You'll come back much more grown up."

"Without rubber pants."

"Rubber pants or no holiday."

Mike recognising an ultimatum gave in, but he roared his disapproval for a full five minutes before George bundled him up to his room.

Sue wheeled herself over to the sofa and eased herself on to it. All children had tantrums and she had some sympathy with Mike's point of view. The twins, according to Sylvia Bray, had done some bed-wetting for a while after starting school. Mike, she said, was probably wetting for the same reason. Provided she had a couple of rubber sheets it would be perfectly easy to cope. Sue wasn't to give it another thought. "It's me," Sue told her. "Before the accident he was perfectly dry." "It's the school," Sylvia contradicted firmly. "It's a stressful time. After another couple of terms he'll be fine."

My neighbours, Sue conceded, are like a school of dolphins edging under me when I'm about to drown and bringing me safely to shore. There were several blessings she had forgotten to tell the unnamed nurse about. Blessings she tended to forget almost as soon as she fleetingly acknowledged them. Especially when the day was grey. Such as now. She hadn't mentioned the visit to George. A peep-show at a paraplegic seemed to sum it up and it was best put out of her mind.

George, after getting Mike into bed and soothing his tears with a story, decided to surprise Sue with the new dress. He had no strong views on it. Tessa had picked out three and modelled them for him. He had sat outside the fitting room feeling a fool and she had come out rather shyly, like a little girl trying party dresses, and stood in front of him and asked him what he thought. He had said "Very nice" about all of them. "But which do you like best?" "Whichever you think Sue would like best. You pick one out." She had chosen a blue one and he had written the cheque and brought it home.

Sue was pouring herself a whisky when he came in with it and her back was turned. "If I were five," she said over her shoulder, "I wouldn't want to wear flaming rubber pants either. How crushed with shame will he be?"

"He'd be more crushed if he wet the bed—which he would. What do you think of this?"

She turned and looked at the dress. "Whose is that?"

"Yours."

84

"It's not. I've never seen it before." She was wary. Enemies, George amongst them, tended at times to creep in the bushes and then emerge to give orders. Wheel your chair down to the bottom of the garden and you'll see the sun through the beech trees . . . Stop being scared of the stairlift, sit on it and get yourself upstairs . . . The cooking stove has been lowered for your use, use it . . . If you want to bath by yourself then use this contraption, but make sure someone is in the house when you do.

She never wanted to bath by herself and it was convenient to let George lift her in and out. She cooked out of shame, and not very well, and usually let George get on with it. She used the stairlift because, like Mike, she had bodily functions and the lavatory was upstairs. As for the sunsets, they were occasionally worth the effort and she occasionally made it.

An effort, she sensed, was going to be required of her very soon. Something to do with the dress.

He told her that he had bought it for her so that she could wear it at the opera on Saturday.

"*You* bought it?"

"With Tessa's help."

That didn't surprise her. The dress looked like Tessa. A blue, silky dress with small flowers on it. The sleeves were batwing.

"Like a butterfly," she said bitterly, "I shall arise from my chair and soar. For God's sake, I'm not going to wear that—it's awful."

"What's wrong with it?"

"Everything. It's—it's coy. Look at me, Mr. Man, I'm a fragile little female. It's a Tessa dress—give it to her."

He tried not to get angry. "Don't be stupid. I can't give it to her. The shop might take it back. What sort of dress *do* you want?"

"I don't know. I don't particularly want one at all. I've still got that green thing. Fetch it down and I'll have a look at it."

He found it in her wardrobe and brought it downstairs. She examined it. It had become shredded under the arms. "This won't do either."

"Then I'll take time off work tomorrow and drive you to the shops. You can choose your own."

She behaved like a hermit crab retiring into␣its shell. He had seen her do it before and knew the moves. The conversation would be changed. "George, could I have a splash more soda in this whisky?"

He put a splash more soda in her whisky.

"Have some yourself. You're looking tired tonight. You must be due for leave soon. When are you taking it?"

He said, "And so on."

"What?"

"And so on. That's the way you always change the subject. I have suggested that I drive you to the shops tomorrow. When we arrive I'll take the wheelchair out of the boot and wheel you around. You can choose the dress yourself."

She drank the whisky contemplatively and then put the glass down. "And how do I try the dresses on?"

"You go into a fitting room and I help you."

"And the sales girls gather around and gently applaud. The legless modom looks perfectly splendid."

George sighed. He had told McKendrick that she had guts—and so she had—but she could also be perversely obstinate and sorry for herself.

"Tessa might get more time off to go with you."

"Damn Tessa!"

He shrugged.

"Look," she said, "I'm sorry. If I go to your opera I'll go as I am."

"*If* you go? I've booked an end-seat for you in the front row. Tessa will be beside you. The toilet, if you need it, is on the ground floor. There are no steps." He didn't say that he had rehearsed for *Otello* for over three months, that he played reasonably well, that though she had heard him practising at home she hadn't heard him with the orchestra, that he wanted her there.

"You are a very practical man, George." It came out sarcastically. "And don't say you have to be. I know you have. Thank you for doing a lavatory reconnaissance—it's nice to know."

She saw his face and relented. "Darling, you're so bloody tired. Come and sit." She took the dress out of his hands and held it in front of her. "Oh, God!" She began to laugh, but with an edge of hysteria. She flung the dress on to the opposite chair. The soft material billowed out like a lady in a swoon.

86

He put his arm around her shoulders. "Shut up and lean against me." He kissed her hair. . . McKendrick, he thought, this is what it's all about.

That night when he carried her from the bathroom and tucked her into bed she pulled his face down to hers and kissed it. "It's just that I don't like being amongst people. I enjoyed the day on the beach. That's why I wanted that particular beach—hardly anyone goes there."

He plumped up her pillow. "But you'll come on Saturday?"

"I'll try to come. Will that do you? I'll try to come."

In that moment he knew she wouldn't. An emotion which he didn't recognise as loneliness touched him like a cold wind. She was lying there in her cocoon of white sheets with her marvellous dark hair spread around her. He stood looking at her, wanting her. She said goodnight gently and turned her head away.

Thirteen

"THE LIBRETTO," HARRIET SAID, MAKING CONVERSA-
tion, "is by Boito, an Italian poet. He was a great admirer of
Shakespeare. Verdi's *Otello* is more of a music-drama than an
opera in the usual sense—or so I've read. I haven't seen it before, have you?"

Ian Mavor hadn't. A short, sharp, cheerful burst of Gilbert
and Sullivan would have been his choice if he had had a choice.
He wondered if Harriet's love of music over-rode her interest in
the story-line. Shakespeare, in Ian's school days, had bored
him to distraction, but he had known what most of the plays
were about. In a last minute effort to have a genuine excuse to
opt out he had tried to swop his on-call duty with Ledman, his
opposite number on Carson's firm, but Ledman wouldn't buy
it.

He moved uncomfortably on the red plush seat. There was
very little leg room. He wanted to smoke, but there were large
'No Smoking' signs on the wall near the stage. You couldn't
sing, he supposed, if you breathed in lungfuls of tobacco. He
wished the theatre manager would announce that the performance was off—a virulent throat bug—anything.

Harriet, aware of his mood without understanding it, asked
him if he liked this sort of thing. He answered that it depended
on the music. The generation gap, non-existent in the hospital,
tended to be very evident out of it. He was behaving meticulously. He had even had his hair cut a little. She wondered if
she should start an animated discussion on cerebral syphilis and

smiled at him with genuine sympathy. "I hope you won't be bored. It was good of you to come."

"It was good of you to ask me."

Bored, he thought? Oh no, Harriet, just a little sick to the gut, that's all.

He had bought her a small box of milk chocolates. "Perhaps you'd like to take the wrapping off before it starts."

She received it gratefully. She loved chocolates. They were part of her weight problem, but she didn't care.

Their seats in the second row were a little close to the orchestra. She noticed that Tessa from the physiotherapy department was in the front row sitting next to an empty seat. She also noticed that when the members of the orchestra came in one of the violinists made a brief gesture of acknowledgement to Tessa and ended it with a shrug. His face was familiar, perhaps he was one of the hospital staff or, even more likely, a former patient. The intensity of her gaze as she tried to place him touched him almost telepathically so that his eyes roved along the rows of seats until he found her.

Doctor Harriet Brand. Consultant anaesthetist. Dressed to the nines in brown velvet with a small upstanding collar of coral pink. Forty-year-old, hefty Harriet, of the wide friendly smile and aura of success. Squired, surprisingly, by Doctor Mavor.

George raised his violin as the lights dimmed for the introductory chorus. And so—sing, he thought bitterly, blast into the rafters with your voices while my puny violin crawls after you. You're not missing a thing, Sue. What difference would it make tonight if you were sitting out there? To hell with the empty seat. The place is full of Harriets and their squires—and their stand-in squires. It was Harriet Brand and McKendrick according to hospital gossip—partners in the operating theatre and partners in bed.

He glanced back at her. Her lips were parted with pleasure as she listened. Next to her Mavor sat, arms folded, as if this were an endurance test, not an entertainment. Or was he thinking of Maggie, perhaps? A very discreet association, that, just beginning to come to light.

The opera, Ian conceded, was well staged. The storm scene was lively. If he could force his mental attitude to be objective it wouldn't be too bad. Otello was recognisable under his make-up as Bill Wharton, an insurance clerk who played a good game of squash. Desdemona was Mary Livingstone of the Nat. West. Bank—her soprano voice just about held its own with Otello's tenor. She didn't at all look like Maggie. These were local townspeople putting on a show. Not badly. In fact, rather well. Relax. Relax.

He looked at his programme in the light from the stage. Cyprus: The end of the fifteenth century. The castle square. After the rumbustiousness of the storm, the fire ensemble and the drinking song—which calmed him—the love duct needled the calm away. He wished the moon would slip from its cardboard sky and fall into the cardboard sea. Illusion. This is all illusion. Keep it out there. Well away. Don't feel anything.

The change of scene for the second act took ten minutes. Harriet, her supply of small-talk muted by a growing knowledge of what she had done, sat in silence. Iago's inciting of the crowd to cry murder had first brought it home to her. Perhaps Ian's silence had nothing to do with identification—perhaps he wasn't steeling himself for what was to come. I'm sorry, she thought, Oh, God, I'm sorry, but what can I do?

She read aloud from the programme. '' 'A hall in the castle.' The scenery is rather good—do you suppose they hired it?''

Ian neither knew nor cared. He said that the general standard of performance was good. It was quite likely that there was enough artistic talent in the company for them to produce their own backdrops.

She couldn't think what else to say. Neither could he. She offered him a chocolate. He took one.

The most outstanding part of the second act was Iago's Credo monologue. The words in praise of evil fell coldly—his sibilants hissed like snakes. Otello's jealous rage in which he vowed vengeance at the end of the scene was less impressive. Over-acted, Ian thought. Keep it that way. Keep shouting and raving and I won't feel a thing.

At the fifteen-minute interval Harriet suggested that they might get themselves a drink. The bar was crowded and they were separated for most of the time while he waited to be served. The five-minute bell sounded when he returned. She took the fruit juice from him and smiled her thanks. "My on-call drink." "Let's hope you won't be called." But he didn't mean it. If she went then he would escort her, thankful to escape.

She guessed what he was thinking and didn't know what to do. Should she be honest and acknowledge the gaffe with an apology and suggest that they should cut the rest of the performance, or keep up the pretence that all was normal? In the end it was easier to do the latter. They went back in.

The violence of Act Three grew gradually with the plotting of Desdemona's death and ending with Otello's emotional collapse. Iago's sarcastic *'Ecco il leone!'* in answer to the off-stage praise of the lion of Venice brought down the curtain.

The interval was short and the light stayed dimmed.

Act Four was the final act and was set in Desdemona's bedroom. Ian looked at the prie-dieu—no Maggie connection there. Humorous—childish—fun-loving—blasphemous little Maggie. The willow-song—not Maggie's music—but it could be. The violins played it sweetly, sadly. It hung in the air like incense and smelt of putrefaction. Don't look at the stage. The leading violinist has a face like a death's-head—or is it the lighting that has drained him of colour? His hand on the bow is strong. He plays well. Very accomplished. Keep thinking of the orchestra—the audience—the hospital—anything.

Desdemona's farewell to her maid.

A change in the music now—deep bass theme.

She's lying on the bed. Otello enters.

Get on with it. Get on with it. Get it over. Suffocation. Not strangulation.

The pillow on her face.

Faithful Desdemona.

Faithless Maggie?

That row about Llewellyn.

A long time ago now.

Everything a long time ago.

Maggie.

Maggie.

God, I love you, Maggie. I love you.

It was eleven-fifteen when Ian drove Harriet home. She had watched him covertly during the latter part of the opera and had willed him to feel nothing. He had sat, too still, his eyes for most of the time averted. In the final burst of applause his hands had begun to tremble and he had held them clenched between his knees. After that he was calm.

They had driven to the opera in her car and as he turned it into her drive she suggested that he might like to come in for a drink. He accepted. She poured him a small whisky and he sat on a green velvet Queen Anne chair and looked around him.

This was reality.

This was the present.

A beautiful home, beautifully furnished. This was the world that went on and handed out rewards if you did your job well—as Harriet did her job well. Harriet, twenty years Maggie's senior, sitting opposite him like a benign and anxious parent. Harriet who had pushed him down dark corridors of the mind, ripped away barriers from scenes that had begun to fade and hoped to smooth it all out again with social chit-chat and a drink.

He sipped his whisky in silence.

Harriet wished she could find the right words that would make him feel better again. One day there would be another girl—and then another. He wasn't built for masochistic self-denial.

A silver-grey tabby inched open the door and padded daintily over the green Chinese rug and jumped on to the sofa. Harriet, grateful for the diversion, went over to it and picked it up. "This," she said introducing him to Ian, "is Lucius Cornelius Sulla Felix—Sulla for short."

Ian dutifully scratched Sulla's head. The cat yawned in deep contentment. He didn't even know the breed of Maggie's dog and he couldn't remember its name. Why were small normal things so elusive? Why did it annoy him so profoundly that certain images refused to form and others formed too easily? Why couldn't one have total control of one's mind? And of one's dreams? Latterly he had slept without nightmares. Harriet had put the spectre at the door again.

"Tonight," Harriet said, "I'm sorry about tonight." She spared him an answer by going on quickly. "Felix walked—according to the old song—a long time ago. Even before my time. The present becomes the past eventually—and the past becomes ancient history. It's no consolation now, I know, but it's a fact. Pain eases. In time it goes."

She repositioned the cat more comfortably in her arms. "He's due for his nightly sniff around the garden. I'll take him out presently. Shall I get you another drink?"

Ian declined. He stood up. "I must be on my way."

"Would you like me to drive you home?"

"No—it's not far. I'll take the short-cut across the Downs."

"Then Sulla and I will walk you down to the gate."

The house abutted the Downs and the garden was full of trees and flowering shrubs. She told him that she didn't like gardening. "This way it's easy—no finicky little flower-beds."

The night wasn't totally dark. The trees were black against a silver grey sky. A waning moon. Milk-white stars.

She bade Ian goodnight and watched as he walked along Beeches Close and turned into Clarence Road. Sulla jumped out of her arms and she followed him slowly down the garden towards the row of conifers that were planted against the wall which separated the garden from the public right of way. It would have saved Ian time had she thought of showing him her own private route to the Downs over the wall and on to the cinder track. Sulla jumped on the wall and embraced a tree, scoring it with long scratch marks. His movements were languid—beautiful—destructive.

She ordered him to stop.

He did so, in his own time.

Paul's dog, she thought, my cat. Whose house—his or mine? Problems. Decisions. She sat for a while on the bench under a lilac tree and let thoughts hum gently through her mind like the lazy buzzing of bees.

The garden smelt strongly of roses. The grass was wet with dew. A bird sang sleepily. She, too, was tired. It was time to go in.

Somewhere behind her she could hear Sulla jumping clumsily—there was a thud—a tearing of leaves.

She called to him without looking around and began walking towards the house.

Paul was awakened at two-thirty by a call from the hospital. There had been a motorway pile-up and two of the patients had serious head injuries. He said he would be along right away. His senior registrar said the switchboard had failed to raise

93

Doctor Brand. It was unlike her not to respond to a call. Paul said he would be passing her house and would look in. They would arrive together. He nearly added, "And make of that what you will."

He wondered what kind of evening she had had with Ian.

When he arrived at her house he saw that the front door was open. Rose petals had blown into the hall and curled like small pink hands on the polished floor. The night seemed suddenly very cold. He searched the house and found Sulla asleep on her bed. It didn't occur to him to search the garden. The hospital had managed to get through to her after their phone call to him, he believed. She had left the house in a hurry. She hadn't closed the front door firmly and the wind had blown it open.

Why did he have this ache of apprehension? All he had to do was to phone the hospital and see if she had arrived.

He used the phone at the bedside.

Doctor Brand wasn't there.

He asked to speak to Ian.

Ian said he'd left her standing by the gate, nursing the cat. "You're urgently needed, sir." His voice was unusually sharp, almost peremptory.

The garden.

The night breeze was like a razor on his skin.

It didn't take him long to find her.

This, too, was a very tidy murder. She wasn't carrying a handkerchief, but she had been cleaned up with a strip of her petticoat which had been folded under her head. Her arms were crossed over her breasts. A large, lovely lady, very peaceful and still.

Harriet depersonalised.

Not Harriet at all.

He refused to believe it.

His bowels were turning to water. He was going to be obscenely sick. By this waxen effigy. By this . . . thing.

He lurched away from her, sweating and moaning and calling her name.

PART
TWO

Fourteen

LIKE A GREAT BEAST UNDER PERSONAL ATTACK THE HOSPI-
tal threw off all vestiges of complacency and became angry and
aware. Sally Gray had been unassuming and pleasant. Maggie
McKendrick scarcely more than a child. Harriet Brand a likeable colleague. The tabloids, intent on sensationalising facts,
had hinted that a psychopath was on the loose. Why should a
maniac pick on the hospital staff? The word 'maniac' began to
be bandied about freely.

The police put out a warning that no woman should be out
late unaccompanied. The hospital re-worded it—no female hospital worker should be out late unaccompanied. It was Rachel
who pinpointed it even further: No member of McKendrick's
neurosurgical team should put herself at risk. Maggie hadn't
been part of his team, but she was his daughter and that was
even closer. She herself regretted that she had applied for the
job of theatre sister, but having got it wouldn't back down. At
the end of Monday afternoon in the theatre she asked McKendrick if she might speak to him.

Normally Paul welcomed new staff and would have made a
point of having a few words with her. As it was, he was finding
it difficult to concentrate on essentials, let along the niceties.
The anaesthetist, William Farrant, was as efficient as Harriet
had been and they had worked together before, but every time
he looked at him he had a gut-twisting memory of Harriet. Harriet dead was still superimposed on Harriet living—like a gro-
tesque negative pinned over a well-loved portrait. Maggie, in

the mortuary, had been presented to him as gently as possible. He had been spared the visual image of the murder and though his mind treacherously created it in his less vigilant moments he had learnt to shy away and not see too clearly what he couldn't bear to see. With Harriet he had seen. He couldn't scrub his mind clean. It was there. Appallingly, shockingly there.

Grief hadn't touched him yet. Nor a sense of loss. When she became Harriet again he would react normally. She would, dear God, become Harriet again. He had to remember Harriet in the body—not just the murdered body of Harriet.

Rachel said, "It's important, sir, that we should speak."

He couldn't think that anything could be important again. Patients were healed—or not healed. The sun rose and set. Just now he wanted to lie down and sleep for a long time.

He took her to his consulting room and told her to sit down. "You're obviously used to theatre work, you did very well." Well—she must have done. He hadn't noticed her.

Now that she wasn't wearing her mask and gown he began seeing her as a person. Young—like all of them. Too young— like all of them. He remembered Sally Gray quite clearly. Mouse-brown hair—good hands. She had done theatre work for six months and then gone on the ward. She preferred personal contact, she had said. She had been useful wherever she was, Sister Gray. And now there was another one. He wished he didn't have to use the name. It was undoubtedly a mistake taking her on.

"Why did you apply for the job?" It came out too sharply and he tried to smooth it over. "I'm not probing, not criticising, it's just that under the circumstances . . ."

"It was because of the circumstances."

He waited wearily for her to explain and then misunderstanding her silence hoped she wouldn't explain. He and Mavor had drawn closer in catastrophe, but Maggie was the common denominator. He was deeply sorry for the girl, but he couldn't take on the additional burden of her grief. Enough was enough.

He said gently, "I liked and respected your sister. Her death was an appalling tragedy and believe me I sympathise with you most sincerely . . ."

She interrupted him crisply. "Condolences are a pain in the

arse. I've crossed streets to avoid them. I'm sorry, sir, but I didn't come here for that.''

It was astringent. He tongued the sour taste of it. "In what way can I help you?''

"Nobody can help me," she said. "And nobody can help you. We're not asking for help, are we? Either of us.''

Get on with it, he thought, whatever it is get on with it.

It came out baldly. "My sister was in your neurosurgical team. She died. Doctor Brand was working with you. She died. Your daughter—the person closest to you—has died. The murders, according to what the papers say, were committed by the same person. I don't think they were indiscriminate.''

The words rasped inside his head and made long grooves of pain. They also made sense. He examined them, tried to obliterate them by pouring scorn on them, and failed.

"Go on.''

She picked up a pencil on his desk, examined the drug advertisement printed on it, and put it down again. "This isn't easy to say. But I have to say what I think. I may be wrong . . . I remember Sally speaking about her patients—'Their gratitude,' she said, 'when things go well is out of proportion to what we do—when things go badly, it swings the other way. It can be very personal. It shouldn't be, but it is . . .' ''

"And so . . . ?''

"And so—your reputation as a surgeon is excellent—and most people know it—but you can't pull miracles out of the sky. Your patients die, too, sometimes, or get worse . . . or just don't get better. There's a pattern to all this and you're at the centre of it. I believe someone thinks you've made a balls-up . . . sorry . . . you've done a bad bit of surgery on someone. It could be a kind of psychotic revenge.''

He tried to make a joke of it. "If that were true, the National Health Service would be even more depleted than it is. No surgeon would dare to operate for fear of failure. I think you're talking a lot of nonsense.''

But he didn't. And she could see he didn't.

"If I am," she said, "then time will prove me wrong. But now we're in the middle of it. I'm fighting for Sally. I won't have her ignored, pushed aside, finished with. In the beginning I was so angry I wasn't afraid. Now I'm still angry, and I'm afraid, too. But that won't stop me." She wondered if she should tell him about her walks in the cemetery and her set-to with the police constable, but decided not to. If he thought her too extreme, too foolhardy, he wouldn't want her in the theatre with him. As yet she hadn't proved her professional ability. She might be afraid to be part of his team, but her reason for joining hadn't changed. She needed to share her knowledge with him and in return hoped he would be a little more forthcoming with her.

She told him that the police had a list of suspects, and watched for his reaction. It was quite obvious he already knew.

She said, "They seem to be looking for a psychosexual pervert."

He knew that, too.

"One of the men listed," she said, "has something to do with the arts. The husband of one of your patients—a paralysed patient—plays the violin for the operatic society. His name is George Webber. I don't know if his name is listed or not. I don't know if he has a normal sex life with his wife or not. I know I can be done for slander for even mentioning him. But I had to tell you. That's what I came to say."

She stood up. "And now, sack me," she thought. "Give me a nice, easy exit. Let me leave this place—this town. Let me survive."

She knew she had shocked him. There was a sudden startled look of recognition in his eyes—a conceding of possibilities—before he had looked away.

He spoke very dryly. "Have you taken this accusation to the police?"

"It isn't an accusation, sir. It's just a thought. I've nothing to go on. I've met his wife. She seems nice—normal—likeable."

He stood up, too. "So you haven't been to the police? To someone else, perhaps?"

"No. I've told no one but you. We're both involved. It's been on my mind for days. You know him. I don't. I just want to be reassured that he's all right . . . that he wouldn't—they've a child, a nice-looking kid, five or so. It's terribly wrong of me to . . . but it's in my head all the time—I keep on thinking about it. I know that sounds silly. I'm not normally indiscreet. If you tell me to stop thinking it—that it's completely out of character—then I promise you I'll never mention it to you or anybody ever again.''

He preceded her to the door. She expected to receive marching orders—a suggestion that she would be of more use to the hospital elsewhere—sorting the dirty linen, perhaps?

He opened it. ''Take my advice, Sister Gray, and leave police matters to the police. I don't have to remind you about loyalties to the patients. Do you want to leave my neurosurgical firm?''

Yes. But she answered, ''No.''

''Then don't have this kind of conversation with me—or with anyone—unless you're totally convinced of your facts.''

It wasn't until after she had left his room and was walking down the corridor that she realised that he hadn't refuted anything she had said.

And that absolves me, she thought. If you're so manacled by a twisted sense of duty towards your patients that you won't move, McKendrick, then I might get a better response elsewhere.

Rumour had it that Ian Mavor had had a thing going for Maggie. Rachel had met him briefly in the operating theatre. They were both off duty that evening and after getting his address from one of the other nurses she called on him at his flat.

He asked her into the small book-littered room without enthusiasm. He wasn't in the mood for socialising with anyone. The police had questioned him for over an hour about Harriet. Maybridge's attitude this time had been subtly different. The first interview had been like a sparring match, the second like the real thing. Blows aimed more carefully drew blood. The dialogue was still very clear in his mind.

Why had he gone to see a particularly evocative opera with Harriet Brand?

Because he had been unable to decline the invitation.

What had been his state of mind as he had sat through it?

Uncomfortable.

Would 'disturbed' be a more accurate description?

Perhaps—but not in the paranoid sense.

Did he have a feeling of antagonism towards Dr. Brand for so insensitively subjecting him to the experience?

No.

Resentment, then?

Possibly.

What had he and Dr. Brand talked about on returning to her home?

Cats—and the passing of time.

Was he being facetious?

No—accurate. (He had repeated the conversation as he had remembered it.)

Had his anger with Dr. Brand aroused revengeful feelings? Had he wanted to hurt her?

No.

Had he wanted to have sexual relations with her—either normally, or otherwise?

No—to both questions.

He had answered that calmly. Had he anticipated the question?

Naturally—in the circumstances.

How much did he know of the circumstances?

What he had read in the newspapers.

Why had the killing taken place in the garden?

He hadn't a direct line to the killer's mind.

After he had left her, what did he do?

After he had left her—alive—at the garden gate, he had walked home.

Had anyone see him?

"I don't know. I hope so."

"So do I, Dr. Mavor. So do I."

And so it had gone on. Gin traps, expertly laid, had invited an incautious step. At the end he had burst out angrily that had he wanted to murder anybody it wouldn't have been Harriet Brand. A mental image of Maybridge spreadeagled on a rack had given him a moment of intense joy. The image might have been projected into Maybridge's mind because Maybridge had looked at him consideringly for a moment or two and then relaxed. The reaction of anger had been the right reaction. Maybridge had pushed him into an emotional outburst and the fireworks had exploded in the right direction. For the time being, Maybridge said, he was prepared to accept the truth of his statements—both verbal and written. No accusation was being made.

102

And now this girl, sitting on the sofa where Maggie used to sit—and lie—and make love—was making the most fantastic accusation he had ever heard.

He listened to it with complete disbelief and told her mildly that she must be potty. "You don't mean to tell me you told McKendrick all this tripe?"

"Yes. And I'd be obliged if you don't tell him I've told you. He doesn't want it spoken about."

"I'm not surprised. I suppose he told you you were talking through the back of your head?"

"No," she said, "he didn't—and that's what worries me. I wanted to be told I was a nutter, but he didn't tell me, and not out of politeness. Oh yes, he told me I was talking nonsense when I first began, but he didn't say it with any conviction. And then when I got on to Webber I could see his reaction. It was like playing darts in a blackout—you don't expect to hit the target. When I left his room I realised I had. I wanted to be told Webber was in the clear. I like his wife. He didn't tell me. If he had I wouldn't be here now. He's a man of High Fine Principles—in capital letters—and he won't have mud slung at anybody, certainly not at the husband of a patient. I don't give a damn to principles and I'll sling mud in any and every direction until I find the man who murdered my sister, even if I get murdered myself."

She spoke the last few words with considerably less conviction than she would have done a while ago. The further one emerged from shock the more one began to like living again.

Ian, recognising the sincerity of her motive, offered to open a can of beer for her. She accepted.

He opened one for himself, too, and began to think over what she had told him. All surgeons had failures. They also had successes that nature came along at a later stage and kicked in the opposite direction. Webber's wife, according to Rachel who seemed to have done her homework, had been operated on two years ago. If one narrowed the field to the last two years there would be perhaps a dozen cases in which a wife or husband, parent or child, was forced to accept what seemed unacceptable. Narrowing the field again to husband, father or son it was still extremely unlikely that one would be a psychosexual pervert as well as a homicidal maniac, and in the right place and at the right time.

Extremely unlikely, but possible.

Rachel's seed of suspicion was capable of producing a plant—not a particularly strong one—but viable for all that. The thesis was sufficiently tenable for a valid argument. It could be taken seriously. All the same it was rough on Webber.

"It would be as well," he told her, "to keep your mouth shut. Webber is one of many—the poor bastard probably had nothing to do with it."

"Oh, I agree," she said, "I agree." She put her can of beer down on one of his text books.

"And if he's already listed as a suspect, then it's up to the police to get on with it." Ian put his empty can of beer beside hers.

"Which of course," she said, "they will."

"But if not . . ." they both voiced it together, and stopped in the same breath.

He asked her abruptly if she were going anywhere that evening. "Or would you like to come round to The Mitre for a drink?"

He hadn't taken a girl out since Maggie's death. He wasn't offering to take this one out in that sense now, but he felt a sudden need for companionship and to talk the matter over further.

She agreed to go.

She saw it as an alliance of the bereaved. A getting together of two people who would make things move. It was a pity, she thought, that McKendrick, the kingpin and possible cause of it all, wasn't throwing his weight in with them.

Fifteen

"AND SO," PAUL SAID, "I WANT YOU TO PUT A TAIL—arrange for surveillance, or whatever you call it—on all my female staff."

It was ten o'clock that same evening and he was sitting in a deep leather chair in Rendcome's study. They had dined together on a well-prepared meal originally intended for two, but which Helen Rendcome had extended to three. "Like the loaves and fishes," she had told her husband in the kitchen, "only in this case it's croissants and soup and a tinned crab salad." She hadn't expected Paul to turn up or, having arrived, to stay. She was a kindly woman, and despite the extra work was glad to have him there. He had eaten very little, but there was nothing she could do about that. The food had to be there in reasonable quantity. The conversation was like pushing a boulder up a hill—he had lost his daughter and his mistress, and how could you compete with that sort of trauma when all you did was to go to the W.I. and the shops and live in fear of getting a parking ticket because your husband was Chief Constable and it Wouldn't Do? She was relieved when Paul told Nigel rather bluntly and not very politely that he would like to speak to him in private and Nigel had taken him into the study.

Nigel sat behind his desk and rested his chin on his hands. "Equally," he said, "I would like you to take all your patients off drug A and put them all on to drug B—which you will administer three times a day."

Paul got the point. "I'm not dictating to you."

"I'm relieved to hear it." He relented. The friendship between them crossed boundaries. It presumed. In Paul's place he would do the same. "For the sake of your peace of mind," he said, "it has already been done."

"Then the theory that we're dealing with revenge killings isn't just so much bullshit?" He had hoped for incredulous laughter when he had come out with the idea, but Rendcome had just sat silently and listened.

Nigel, who chose his words more fastidiously, said that in a murder case where a pattern seemed to be establishing itself one covered every possibility. "Did this man Webber threaten you?"

"No, but I've told you he's under considerable stress. I should have been a miracle worker. I should have cured his wife. They don't sleep together—had I performed the operation with more expertise, according to his insinuations, she would be normal in every way."

"A more logical revenge would be to castrate you on a dark night."

"Who's talking about logic?"

Nigel drew a series of boxes on his blotter and then drew a line through them. "Neither of us. It makes a mad sort of sense, I suppose. I don't know who put this idea into your head—perhaps it just grew there. At least you've come to me with it, not to anybody else. You're walking on extremely dangerous ground. The laws of the land protect the private individual—as you know."

"Is this particular private individual on your list?"

"No," Rendcome said, "he isn't." He had been prepared for the question and it came out flatly.

Paul looked at him keenly. Nigel held his gaze. The lie—like something they could pick up and examine—lay between them.

"I have a great regard," Nigel said stiffly, "for our friendship. Get on with your own job. Keep out of mine. All the hospital staff were interviewed after Maggie's murder. The same thing is happening again now. And not just the hospital staff—a good proportion of the townspeople as well. You've given me a name. You've given me a theory. Before this case is solved I'll have been given a few dozen names—a few dozen theories. The

106

name and the theory will eventually match and when they do I'll tell you.''

And in the meantime, Paul thought, can you imagine the weight of my own personal guilt? He wished to God he had never set eyes on Rachel Gray. Until a few hours ago he had had—not peace of mind—but an easy conscience. The maniac, whoever he might be, hadn't been triggered into a rampage of murder due to his own shortcomings, or imagined shortcomings. On his way here tonight Paul had driven over to the Romney Hill estate and parked at the end of the road where Webber lived. Neat little houses. Neat little lives? He couldn't go thrusting his way in with accusations. He just didn't know. It was possible, even likely. But yet it wasn't fact. So hold on to your cool. Drive away. Hand it over to Nigel. Be patient. Be openminded. Be *calm*.

Before he left, Nigel took him through to the sitting room for some of Helen's excellent coffee. She and her husband sat together on the sofa. In an unthinking moment she rested her head against his shoulder and then saw Paul's glance and moved away. Sorry, she apologised silently, sorry.

It was in that moment that he began seeing Harriet again—the living Harriet, as she had been. The distortion and the horror faded and the memory was clear and sweet. He waited for the pain and when it came hugged it to him. Helen said something, but he didn't hear. She looked at Nigel, her eyes wide with distress. He shook his head gently at her. This was part of friendship, too. The part where you sat and did nothing, where your gift was the gift of silence.

The following morning Rendcome called a conference of his senior officers. Out of an ocean of hard graft was thrown up what could be a red herring or a useful piece of evidence. The ground around Harriet had been damp and the grass had been flattened by a long, fairly heavy object. The police photographer had done his best under difficult circumstances and the photographs were reasonably clear. ''The danger,'' Rendcome said, ''is to chip and chisel away at a possibility and trim it up into a fact. It could be an impression made by a violin case— and it could be one of a dozen other objects. Why would a violin case be carried to the scene of the crime? Would the murderer climb the garden wall, violin case in hand? Why not leave it on the Downs side of the wall? Why not leave it in the car? Why a violin case at all?''

Detective Superintendent Claxby let the Chief Inspector answer that one. Maybridge explained that one of his sergeants, Stannard, had noticed the highly polished state of Webber's violin case, in an otherwise unpolished and tatty domestic environment, on the day following Maggie McKendrick's murder. She, too, had been murdered on a showery evening.

He added dryly, ''That particular gem of information was imparted with a show of extreme reluctance. Stannard and Webber are neighbours. Stannard's wife spends a great deal of her time at the Webbers'.''

Rendcome, aware that Stannard's motives might not be ascribed wholly to his devotion to his job, nevertheless was prepared to accept them at face value. They had nothing else to go on. He asked if the photographs of Maggie's murder and Sally Gray's murder had shown a similar flattened area of grass.

They hadn't.

''When you begin to point the finger,'' he said, ''you point it with some certainty. If Webber can't prove he wasn't in the vicinity of the Brand murder then let the forensic people have a look at his violin case. In the first place, request it. The evidence so far is extremely thin. Interrogate him here—it's a less cosy atmosphere than the hospital. I want the interview on tape.'' He would have liked to sit in on it, but knew it wouldn't be good policy.

The Press Officer was Chief Inspector Powell. ''Keep the public happy,'' he told him, ''by saying that investigations are making some headway. No names. No hints. Unless you'd like to say the police are playing it by ear.'' He smiled at his own joke and the others smiled dutifully, too.

Claxby, highly sceptical of the revenge theory, said that the urologist had made a balls-up of his father's prostate operation, and that he had been a clarinettist in his youth. Laughter this time was spontaneous. ''If I were pointing the finger,'' Claxby went on, ''I'd be more inclined to point it in the direction of Mavor. You're assuming he's sexually normal. You're assuming he's mentally well balanced. You could be wrong.''

''Naturally, he's not ruled out,'' Maybridge said crisply

"But I've been in contact with enough nutters in my time to smell them several miles off. Mavor is your typical twenty-four-year-old, naïve, occasionally canny, healthy procreator of the species. But Webber . . . he's something else again. Ever since my first interview with Webber I've had this feeling."

"As long as your 'feeling' doesn't amount to prejudice," Rendcome told him, "carry on with the interrogation yourself. If it does, delegate it."

The interview room at the police station was painted a pale shade of green. It was sparsely furnished with a table, two wooden chairs with leather seats, and a metal cabinet. An electric clock indicated that the time was two twenty-five. Maybridge, who had asked George to be there by two o'clock, still hadn't arrived.

The softening-up process, George brooded. Apprehension grows as the time ticks by. I am probably being observed. We will, of course, be tape-recorded.

He felt nothing more than a frozen embarrassment. All the Maggie McKendrick interviews had been held at the hospital. His interview had been one of many. True, he had had the honour of being interrogated by Maybridge, but he hadn't been the only one. As far as he knew, he was the first member of the hospital staff to be interviewed here. It hadn't been easy to think up a plausible excuse to tell his colleagues why he had to leave the department in the early part of the afternoon. At least they hadn't sent a squad car for him. They had allowed him to drive here himself.

He had a headache and needed an aspirin. He had a flat packet of them in his wallet and took it out. He couldn't swallow without water and they were distinctly unpleasant to chew. If he were being observed they would think he was drugging himself or poisoning himself. That might bring them rushing in. He took two tablets out of their wrapping and ate them slowly, grimacing at the after-taste.

Sue could swallow without difficulty.

What are you doing now, Sue, in the middle of the afternoon? Writing to Mike, perhaps. You almost cried when you waved him off. He forgot to wave, he was too taken up with

109

that awful dangling monkey hanging from the car window. Homesick? Not Mike. He'll have the time of his life.

Maybridge, at the door, said, "I'm sorry to have kept you waiting." He noticed the packet of aspirin but did not comment. "It was good of you to come."

George asked dryly, "I had a choice?"

Maybridge sat opposite him. "If you had a good reason to decline the invitation I might have listened to it."

"I am 'helping the police'?"

"It's a useful phrase—you needn't translate it too literally at this stage—or rather, give it its true meaning, not what it has come to mean."

He began with the Sally Gray murder, referring when necessary to the sheaf of notes he had brought in with him. "On that particular night you had also been attending a rehearsal of *Otello*, but you returned home by car. You stated that you were in the house at eleven-fifteen. There were no witnesses to your time of arrival. We accepted your statement; there seemed no reason not to."

"But there is now?" George moved his long legs impatiently and caught the corner of the table with his foot. "Sorry." He could still taste the aspirin and took out a cigarette.

"I don't know. There might be." Maybridge clicked his lighter and leaned over with the flame.

George asked, "We're being tape-recorded?"

"Why should you think that?"

"Your w.p.c. note-taker isn't around."

"Yes, we're being tape-recorded."

Maybridge referred to the notes again. "On the night of Margaret McKendrick's murder you returned from the rehearsal on foot. You sat on the Downs. You were quite woolly about the time you arrived home. On the first occasion you said quite precisely eleven-fifteen. On the second occasion you didn't know with any certainty. You were not—and I'm quoting you— 'obsessional about time. My mind was on the rehearsal,' you said, 'it was probably somewhile after twelve.' When I pressed you to be more definite, you said, 'Well, before one.' It was interesting that you should mention one o'clock."

"That, I suppose, was the murder time?" The conversation

110

was almost academic. George felt totally uninvolved. His head was still throbbing.

"It can't be exactly pinpointed, but your time on the Downs can be. We have interviewed a young couple in a car. They saw you sitting on the bench overlooking the estuary. They particularly remembered your violin case. The fact that you were there they probably found inhibiting. You got up and left at twenty minutes past twelve. You walked in the direction of the copse. The path through the trees would have led you eventually to the wasteland where Maggie McKendrick was found."

"Equally the left fork is a shortcut to Wedmore Street. I didn't go near Buttress Way."

"Accepting your word on that—for the time-being—did you see anyone going in the opposite direction—towards the wasteland?"

"No."

"You're not a very observant man, Mr. Webber. In your previous statement you didn't see the young couple either . . . Do you want to change your statement now and admit that you did?"

A murder suspect—possibly a voyeur—a woolly-minded lunatic who never bothered to look at his watch. It was all unnecessarily complicated and stupid. He decided to stick with his original statement.

"I didn't see anyone."

Maybridge didn't press it. "You stated that you went up Wedmore Street possibly somewhile after twelve and saw some youngsters from a disco. You didn't describe them in any detail. One—a quite striking young Pakistani—remembered a man carrying a violin case. She remembered the time clearly enough because she was in a panic about being late home. It was one twenty-five. So you remember her?"

"No." He did, of course. Did Pakistanis wear decorative bracelets on their ankles? When he wrote the statement accuracy had seemed to matter. Indian, or some other culture? It had seemed important then to know. His head still wasn't easing much. Usually aspirin worked fairly fast.

He asked mildly, "Are you accusing me of murdering Maggie McKendrick?"

111

"I'm accusing you of being totally misleading in your timing of events."

"I beg your pardon. As from now I'll do everything by the clock." It was a mistake. He apologised again. "I didn't mean to be flippant."

Maybridge's lips tightened a little. "It's understandable. You're under stress."

Am I? George wondered. Apart from his head and a general feeling of fatigue he felt no stress whatsoever. Maybridge—the interview—the room—were like something lifted out of television. The fact that he was pushed into the role of actor caused him no apprehension at all. His lines were somewhere in the back of his head; all he had to do was to trot them out. Too bad if they were occasionally the wrong lines. He waited for the rest of the scene.

Maybridge picked up a fresh sheaf of notes. "As you know, Doctor Brand was murdered on the night of the performance of *Otello*. The cast of the opera—including, of course, the orchestra—celebrated a successful evening by throwing a backstage party which went on until midnight or so. You didn't attend. Why?"

"I'm not a particularly gregarious person. I enjoy music rather more than I enjoy the company of musicians." (I would have stayed had you been there, Sue. As my wife you would have been welcome. The place was stiff with married couples.)

"So what did you do?"

"I drove home."

"Immediately?"

"As you know I didn't stay for the party, you probably know that I didn't drive home immediately."

"Go on."

"I'm under surveillance, I suppose?"

It would be better for you if you were, Maybridge thought, one way or the other. If you were, the Brand woman might be alive.

"No, you haven't been under surveillance, but as you're probably discovering we are our brothers' keepers to a certain extent. It would be as well now to start with the truth. Where did you go?"

112

George almost smiled. "Would you believe me if I said on the Downs?"

Maybridge said levelly, "Yes, I'd believe you. Now tell me where on the Downs, and why?"

Where was easy. "I parked my car near the intersection of Clarence Road and Mayberry Avenue, and then I took the footpath that looks over the river." *Why* wasn't so easy. It was almost impossible. "Night time is a quiet time—I need to withdraw from a musical experience gradually. Does that make sense to you?"

It could do, Maybridge thought, given a different set of circumstances. Mayberry Avenue was ten minutes away from Beeches Close, where Doctor Brand lived. It was curious that he should admit to being so near. Perhaps this time he had seen someone or been seen. He asked him.

"There might have been people around. I didn't notice."

"And—of course—you didn't notice the time?"

"No."

"When you took your walk, did you carry your violin case?"

There's an error in the script, George thought. Why talk about violins?

"Of course not. Why should I burden myself with my violin case?"

Maybridge looked back through his notes. "On February the fifteenth this year you reported to the police that your car had been broken into. A briefcase was stolen from the back seat. After that sort of experience it's likely that you would carry anything valuable with you."

"I could have locked it in the boot."

" 'Could have' isn't definite. Did you?"

George hesitated. What was the right answer to this one? He decided on the affirmative. "Yes, I locked it in the boot."

"Would you have any objection to our having a look at your violin case?"

"A look at it . . . ? Oh I see. Your forensic people. I wasn't aware that Harriet Brand had been battered to death with a violin case." If this wasn't so bloody funny I might start taking it seriously.

Maybridge was looking at him curiously. Nothing is getting through, he thought. Your mind is locked away. You're not

113

giving it any intellectual consideration. To you it's a macabre sort of game. There was no history of mental aberration. He had had no breakdown. Given that his home conditions were difficult, he appeared to have coped. Up to now.

Maybridge stood up. "All right—shall we go?"

George frowned, not understanding. Go? Where? To the cells? To the scaffold? Back to the hospital? For a drive on the Downs?

"Go where?"

"To your home. To pick up your violin."

"Oh, now—wait a minute." Reality began rolling in like a thundercloud. Home was where Sue was. Was he expected to walk in with this idiot of a policeman and tell Sue that his violin was to be gone over by the forensic people in a search for blood-matted hairs? He said, "Harriet Brand was murdered in the same way as the other two. She was strangled. If you didn't want me to know that then you shouldn't be so liberal with your press hand-outs. It's in the newspapers. What has my violin to do with any of it?"

Maybridge was soothing. "Possibly nothing, but we won't know until we have it."

"I won't have my wife disturbed—worried—by something so incredibly stupid. Play me along as much as you like, but keep her out of it."

Maybridge acknowledged to himself that Webber's concern for his wife was genuine. Bearing in mind that the Chief Constable would very shortly have the tapes played back to him, he wondered if he would be censured for leniency at his next suggestion. "I'm not in uniform. We'll use your car. I shall have to come in with you, but you needn't disclose my identity. You can tell her you are lending the violin to me."

It was fair to the point of being unprofessional. Later, when the evidence was more solid, he would be totally professional; but as yet no charge could be made.

Sue was playing Scrabble when they arrived. When playing against herself it was possible to cheat and she used the dictionary freely. Zambuk, she had discovered, was New Zealand slang for a first-aid man. Her mind was on hospital matters and she thought that George had returned early with a colleague from the hospital. She hoped he wouldn't want tea. There were

114

scones in the tin, but they were two days old. Even with a smothering of butter they would taste stale. She said something vague about a drink.

Maybridge declined.

She was a lovely woman. A strand of hair had come loose and curled over her shoulder. Her feet in open-toed brown sandals were bare. Useless feet, he remembered. Some of the words on the Scrabble board he had never heard of, but he stopped himself commenting on them. The room around her was in total disorder, but she seemed quite unaware of it. She would, he guessed, be just as indolent if she were not confined to her chair. According to medical reports she could give her husband sexual satisfaction—and by God, looking at her, he could imagine it. According to McKendrick her libido was dead. Difficult to believe.

The violin case was propped up in a corner by the bookcase. As Stannard had commented, it was the only thing in the place that had had any polishing. It shone like a sleek black seal. It was doubtful if the forensic tests would turn up anything incriminating on it. He told George that he kept it in good condition.

"Next to me," Sue joked, "it's his greatest love." It surprised her that George should lend it to anyone. That he was lending it with great reluctance was perfectly obvious. She thought he looked ill and wondered if he had a cold coming on. He had been tired and strained since the night of the concert. His disappointment when she had refused to go with him had been out of all proportion. Unusually for her she had been asleep on the sofa when he had returned and had awoke in his arms when he was carrying her upstairs. She had told him sleepily that he smelt of grass—the green sort that grew. Afterwards, in the bathroom, she asked him about the concert. He was handing her the towel and there were grass stains on his fingers. He had said it was rosin and she was too sleepy to argue. There had been bitter lines around his mouth, but he had kissed her with his usual gentleness when he had carried her through to the bedroom and put her in bed.

The opera had been very good, he had told her. The murder of Desdemona had been excellent.

115

Sixteen

TESSA, QUIET AS A NUN, BUT NOT BREATHLESS WITH ADO-
ration, lay stiffly on her back and listened to what Louis had to
say. They had copulated—an animal word which befitted an animal act. She had watched it happen many times on the Galway
farm and had once been cuffed around her ear by her mother for
taking an unhealthy interest. "Get away with you, child, in the
name of God!" Her mother's voice could be strident and her
hand rough and leathery. But there had been a lot of love between them. Later, she had confessed it to the priest. "Father, I
saw a cock and a hen make love, and two pigs, and a dog and a
bitch." Cats were more discreet: she had never caught them at
it. The priest had told her to say three Hail Marys and to thank
God for the holy act of creation. She hadn't known what the last
part meant, but his voice had shaken with merriment when he
told her.

There was nothing funny about Louis's love-making. He was
sitting, naked, on the side of the bed, his skin beaded with
sweat. If his grunts and groans were anything to go by, he had
enjoyed himself.

Now, he appeared to be deranged. She had never heard him
talk such nonsense in her life.

"I'm not ordering you not to go there anymore," he told her.
"You're a grown woman, but if you've got any sense you'll listen to me."

She said stiffly, "He's the most gentle man I know."

So he had hurt her. He was sorry, but it had served her right.

116

The fact that she suffered his advances in the truest sense of the word and turned her blue eyes ceilingwards with pious resignation exasperated him beyond endurance.

He spoke harshly. "How does he do it then? To the strains of the violin? Swing low, sweet chariot, while I swing it into you?"

She winced at his coarseness. "He's never touched me."

He wished he could believe her. If Webber couldn't have it with his wife and there was a lady ready and willing across the road . . . ? A lady from an Irish bog farm who had once, a long time ago, sold him eggs when he had camped in her father's field. Her legs had been the colour of honey and her breasts small like mushrooms. To deflower her, as she had quaintly put it, had been part of the holiday scene. He hadn't intended taking the flowerless maiden home after honourably marrying her. Her innocence, her naïvety, had amused and disarmed him. He had wanted to marry her. He had wanted to care for her—permanently. He still did.

He began rubbing himself with a towel. "The police are working on Webber. They won't take him into custody until they have more proof." He noticed that he had used the word 'they' rather than 'we'. All right—so he was trying to disassociate himself from something that would make her dislike of him grow even more. They. The fuzz. That rough lot of men where he worked. "They're doing forensic tests on his violin."

"On his—what?" She sat up, astonished. She thought he must be joking and then saw that he wasn't.

He told her what he shouldn't have told her, only he made it sound a lot more definite. The shadow on the photograph was an indentation made by the pressure of a violin case on damp grass—not *might be*—but *was*.

She didn't believe any of it. It was a horror story that had sprung out of his twisted imagination. If anyone were a psychosexual pervert it was Louis himself. So far he had behaved within the acceptable rules of the game—game . . . this? But the undercurrent of violence reached through to her spine. Love with George would be a union full of happiness. She had read books about it, and poems. Her body in George's presence—even though they never touched—responded with a strong sexual awareness. She closed her eyes sensuously thinking of him.

117

Louis looked at her with disgust. "All right," he said. "Keep going there. Keep skivvying for them. But don't be shocked when your honourable, gentle, parfait knight gets what's coming to him." He tried to level the anger out of his voice. "Be careful, Tessa."

She opened her eyes and looked at him. His concern pricked the bubble of her dream. Don't care about me, she thought, please don't care. I want to be free.

The reason for his concern was too idiotic for serious thought. He was always trying to goad her. She hadn't realised until now that his jealousy of George ran so deep.

He began to dress. It was six o'clock in the evening and he was due back on duty. She would, he knew, be very pleased about that. She would have the bed to herself tonight—all night. He wondered if she knew just how tired he was—how tired they all were. In the normal way he would be spending an hour at the shooting range and then coming home. He hadn't told her he had been issued with a gun. He would have liked to boast about it, but could only too easily imagine her reaction. In any case, he had probably divulged too much already.

After he had gone Tessa baked a sponge cake and took it across the road to Sue. The cake was still warm in its tin and she put it on the kitchen table. George was washing up the accumulated dishes of the day. This, Tessa nearly told him, you shouldn't have to do. Sue is perfectly capable of wheeling herself into here and getting on with it. She was wise enough not to voice the criticism, and instead helped to dry the dishes and put them away.

George accepted her help with some show of polite gratitude. On this particular evening he would have preferred a quiet period in the kitchen on his own. He kept going over the interview with Maybridge but couldn't remember what had been said—and implied—in any order. In retrospect it was like an amalgam of Mike's large wooden jigsaw puzzles. You picked up a piece and examined it and wondered which picture it belonged to. Normally your mind clicked along obediently and—one, two, three—a pattern emerged. The piece that represented his violin case refused to slot in anywhere. Was it the first sign of madness to think that others were mad?

Tessa was saying something about jam.

118

"Where do you keep it?" She was looking in the store cupboard. "I want to slice the cake through and spread some on."

Sue, overhearing from the living room, looked up from her book and called out that they were out of it. "There's lemon curd." She wished Tessa would leave the cake and go away.

Tessa found the lemon curd. She spread it carefully. "If you'd like to make a list of anything else you're short of I'll do some shopping for you tomorrow."

George said, "Thanks," briefly, but made no effort to make a list.

Tessa, her eyes warm with concern, touched his hand. "Are you all right?"

"Of course." It was sharp, snappy. He tried to smile at her. "A busy day at work, that's all. Sue will make you a list sometime."

They went into the living room together and Sue closed her book and dropped it on the floor beside her. She had been reading Wilde's *The Birthday of the Infanta* and found it singularly depressing. Tessa picked it up and put it away tidily on the bookshelf. "What's it about?"

"A dwarf with twisted legs. He's in love with a princess." Sue waited for the "Oh?" and embarrassed silence that would follow it.

Tessa followed the silence with, "He was a homosexual, wasn't he? Wilde, I mean?"

"Yes." And I don't want to talk about him. Go home, Tessa, go home to your lusty Louis. There's something between George and myself tonight—like a grey wall of fog. I don't know what it is. I'm afraid to know. But I've got to know.

Tessa sensed her mood. She remembered what Louis had said about the violin. It wasn't in the room, and through the open door she could see it wasn't in the hall. She suggested that they might have some music. On other evenings they had done this. She could manage simple tunes on the piano, and Sue, when she could be bothered, could accompany the violin with the more difficult pieces.

George said that he had lent the violin to a colleague from work.

"Oh, then Louis . . ." Tessa broke off and began smiling broadly. "Honestly, he's a complete fool."

119

When Sue asked her what she meant she refused to answer. "Nothing—forget it—it's just too stupid." She changed the subject. "How is Mike enjoying his holiday with the twins?"

"Enormously. He's not missing us one bit."

They had talked about Mike. About the possibility of a family holiday later on with Sue's parents in the Midlands. About Louis's leave being cancelled on account of the murders. "He wanted to go to Spain—I didn't. I can't say I mind too much staying at home." (Near you. Can you guess what I'm thinking? I hope not. It's good just to be here tonight, helping in any way I can. Your shirt's crumpled. Doesn't Sue ever iron them? You've made everything so easy for her to lead a fairly normal life. A dwarf with . . . did she know it was that sort of story when she started it? Do you *ever* go to bed together?)

George felt the time grinding by. Ten o'clock. Go, woman, go. Oh, you're kind, Tessa, kind. We don't deserve you—either of us. But go—please God—go.

She went at ten-fifteen after making them all some coffee and giving them a slice of cake.

Sue, in a moment of remorse, gave her a quick good-night kiss. "Thanks for everything."

George saw her to the door.

She paused at the garden gate. "You'll call me if you want me—any time?"

Yes, he said, he would call her if he wanted her any time.

It's difficult, Sue discovered, to walk through a wall of fog and walk in the right direction. It also takes courage.

She began tentatively. "It was quite a gaffe—but she covered it quickly."

"What do you mean?" But he knew what she meant. He began busying himself with the cups and plates.

She told him to put them down. "We've got to talk."

"Have we? About what?"

"That man, this afternoon, the one you gave the violin to. Who was he?"

"Maybridge." He couldn't protect her if she refused to be protected, so he gave him his full title. "Detective Chief Inspector Maybridge."

"And Louis knew about it and mentioned it to Tessa?"

"Obviously."

She was in the middle of the fog now—afraid—but still walking. "Tell me why."

He told her about the interview, but tried to make light of it. "I'm one of many—it's just police routine. It happened after Sally Gray and Maggie McKendrick—now it's Harriet Brand. The police have to do their job." He drew up his chair opposite hers. There was a cake crumb at the side of her lip. He wanted to wipe it away, but this wasn't a moment for touching. He felt frozen in his chair.

"But why the violin? Why should the police want the violin?"

He told her that he didn't know.

"What did that man—Maybridge—ask you?"

He gave her a carefully edited version of the interview as he remembered it.

"But it doesn't make any sense. Why should you be connected in any way with psychopathic killings—they are that, aren't they? That's what the newspapers hint."

"I don't know." But this time he did know, but couldn't tell her.

She was aware of the quickening of her heartbeat as she herself began to know. The journalists had made several suggestions—someone who was sexually deprived being one of them.

"I see," she said, "Oh, God . . ." She felt sick.

He told her calmly enough that she didn't see anything. "I love you. The fact that I don't sleep with you doesn't turn me into a sex-starved killer."

She reached out her hands and touched his. But how would they know they didn't sleep together? Why jump to that conclusion when there was no physical reason for it? McKendrick had made it clear that she could have children. She remembered the grass stains on his hands after the night of the opera. He had smelt of grass. Perhaps he had had a prostitute—out of doors somewhere, in the darkness. If so, why not tell the police and be done? She could accept it. She had to accept it.

Her fingers tightened on his as she told him.

He withdrew his hands.

"I went on to the Downs. I sat for a while. I walked. That's all."

"Darling, don't be afraid to hurt me. I won't be hurt. It's nat-

121

ural. I don't mind. If you need an alibi—and you've been with someone—then don't be afraid to say. It's you—not me—now. Stop thinking about me."

As easy as willing the earth off its orbit.

She said in sudden fury, "You can't just accept their appalling accusations. You can't turn me into something—" she cast around for the word "—sacrosanct. It's you—damn you—who's at risk."

He tried to calm her. "Not just me. I haven't been set up for special treatment. Why they wanted my violin is a mystery. And there have been no accusations." He didn't add "yet".

She sensed the omission and was even more afraid. He had been late home on several occasions. He had tried to mislead her about the time. There must be someone. He wouldn't walk on the Downs at night just for—what? Repose of the soul? Dear sweet Jesus!

If not a prostitute—then who? Certainly not Tessa. It was becoming increasingly obvious that Tessa was sick with love of him, but it wasn't reciprocated. He was completely indifferent to her.

After the nightly ritual of tucking her into bed and leaning over to kiss her, she held his face in her hands and explored his mouth with her tongue. Her face was very pale and cold. He could feel her trembling and held her close. It was a valiant effort on her part, but was so obviously effort that he felt no stimulus whatsoever. He could have cried for both of them.

She was crying, "I'm sorry. Very, very sorry."

"Hush, my love. My sweet."

"Do you think you could just lie with me?"

He told her roughly, no. And then kissed her again gently and with closed lips.

"If anyone is mad," she said, "it's me. I probably need therapy. McKendrick doesn't deal in libido, does he? Just legs. Do you think if he had another go at mine he'd make me feel?" The old hope of another operation loomed up and began to take shape. "Do you think if I saw McKendrick again he might be able to help me—even just a little?"

He hadn't told her that he had been to McKendrick recently and with the same question.

He told her now, breaking it to her as gently as he could.

122

"I see—so he's done all he can." She accepted it.

He couldn't. Yes, he thought, he's done all he can, and there you lie as proof of it.

He went to the bathroom and returned with her sleeping tablets. Tonight she needed them. Tonight she wouldn't demure. She took them without a word of protest.

On the far side of the fog was a bleak, barren landscape. She walked through it in her sleep and felt the grass-denuded soil like ash on her feet.

Seventeen

IAN MAVOR WAS THE FIRST PERSON PAUL TOLD ABOUT THE reward. "I thought two thousand for any information leading to an arrest." He had invited Ian back to his home to pick up some text books and have a drink. He had noticed the growing friendship between Ian and Rachel and felt a degree of jealousy on Maggie's behalf. Did the young forget so easily? Was it forgetting or a getting together in a common cause? If the latter, what good could they hope to do? Money thrown into the ring might bring results. He could afford it. He wondered why he hadn't thought of it before.

Ian was slowly learning to be at ease in Paul's presence. (What kind of father-in-law would he have been? Too possessive of Maggie, perhaps—too ambitious for Ian's success?) These were academic questions now, the answers didn't matter. Rachel was a spitting, biting little alley cat compared with Maggie, but she was making him feel normal again. He no longer anaesthetised himself with work. Laughter was becoming a gut response again. The world could be funny at times. Hilarious, even. He stopped having horrific visions and dreaming appalling dreams. He and Rachel could quarrel with some passion. It was nice to be able to care about stupid things once more. Grief could be engulfing. You had to fight your way free.

He said that he thought the reward was a good idea. He then risked telling Paul about Rachel's vendetta theory, and then remembered that he already knew.

Discretion, Paul was learning, wasn't one of Rachel's finer points, and he might be unwise to tell Ian that the police had gone through his records to find out how many patients might be the cause of a personal vendetta. It was a salutary experience. Failures, on the whole, were few and far between, but when you began totting them up it seemed an excellent idea to sling your scalpel into the waste-bin and have an early retirement. The police had narrowed the field to three. Two, when questioned, had thoroughly water-tight alibis. The third was Webber.

He decided to tell Ian. "The theory is far-fetched to the point of being ludicrous, but the police take everything seriously—even that." He didn't add: And so do I, God help me. He kept on seeing Webber's face just before he had gone storming out of his consulting room. The coffee stain on the wall was a constant reminder. Hospital funds didn't cover redecoration until a given number of years had passed. It was easier to offer two thousand pounds reward than to give the hospital administrators fifty quid to slap some emulsion on the wall. There were times when he felt like quitting England—even quitting the job altogether. A stint as a deck-hand at sea would be therapeutic. Only, who would take him on? A fifty-one-year-old neurosurgeon who had been twice traumatised and would carry the cicatrix to the end of his days.

He tried to joke about it. "I don't suppose you feel like taking up general practice? You just put the buck on a conveyor belt and it whizzes off to whichever poor devil of a specialist you aim it at."

Ian answered loyally and with complete sincerity. "You're the best man in your field. If you couldn't cure Mrs. Webber, no one could."

"Try telling Webber that."

It was only recently that Ian had discovered what Webber looked like. Rachel had pointed him out in the hospital canteen. She had wanted to go and sit at his table. "We'll get his reactions. Ask him who he thinks has done it." He had stopped her. "In the Middle Ages, you would have baited bears." "Yes, and made them damn well dance. What's the matter with you— don't you want to know?" "Of course I want to know. But the police are getting on with it." It was reassuring news that they had gone through McKendrick's files. There seemed no reason why he shouldn't tell Rachel and warn her to keep quiet about it. They had wanted things to move. They were moving.

They were moving, from the Chief Constable's point of view, at a manageable pace. He tried to dissuade Paul from offering a reward. "We'll be swamped with telephone calls—letters—personal visits—mostly from time-wasters. Wait a while. Don't clog the works."

But Paul refused to wait. "It's already several weeks since the murder of Sally Gray. The same thing will happen with Maggie and Harriet. If you can't cope cancel leave, take on more staff."

Nigel held on to his temper. "We have already cancelled leave. There's no more staff to take on. You beef about your housemen working an eighty-hour plus week. What do you suppose my men are doing?" In the end he had to concede that it was Paul's privilege to do what he liked with his money. "But if you give a press conference, be careful."

It hadn't occurred to Paul to give a press conference. That, too, was a good idea. It was arranged for the following Friday afternoon and was held in his consulting room. The reporters, notebooks at the ready, turned up in force. There weren't enough chairs. He pushed his desk against the wall to give them additional space and delivered his speech standing.

He didn't dramatise anything. He wasn't emotional. He just said clearly and reasonably that there could well be someone somewhere who could come forward with vital information about anything concerning one or all of the murders. He urged the public to think about the dates in question. Questions adroitly angled by the pressmen elicited responses he hadn't intended. He had had no intention of urging the public to examine its conscience. It hadn't been his intention to plead with the public to stop shielding a husband—a brother—a son—who might have unnatural tendencies. Rhetorical questions bounced off him in the direction the reporters intended them to bounce. The spoken word, deftly manipulated, made good emotional impact. Descriptions made even better impact. He had believed he had himself well in hand and was commendably calm. The newsmen didn't see it that way. He was described as a heartbroken father crushed with a weight of grief. (Fortunately the papers didn't describe him as a heartbroken lover pining for his dead mistress, but they probably would have, had they known.)

The following morning he read the various newspaper reports with alarm and horror and could have flung them at Nigel when he said with some asperity, "Well, what did you expect?"

"Certainly not this."

"But you've got it. Perhaps as from now you'll listen to me."

Rachel read the newspaper reports with delight. McKendrick had done very well indeed. One would never have guessed by his air of clinical detachment that he had it in him. If this didn't bring everyone running nothing would. She was waiting in Ian's flat for him to come off duty. Unlike Maggie she never bothered to cook for him, but she kept the place reasonably tidy. His books were in neat piles and grouped according to subject matter. He studied usually early in the morning and found this useful. He also found the duvet useful. It had appeared suddenly and he had received it without comment. Rachel and her bedding had come to stay for a while. She wasn't Maggie, but he quite liked having her around. Rachel, sensing that the relationship could deepen, bided her time. They were good for each other. He might not admit it and she certainly didn't voice it, but they were.

When he came in she flourished the papers at him. "Look—your high and mighty McKendrick's absolutely super."

He read the accounts and shuddered. "He'll sue them for misrepresentation." And then he looked at Rachel and began to laugh. It didn't seem possible that there was anything remotely funny in such an appalling tragedy, but there was. He sat on the sofa and howled with laughter. She kneed him in the stomach, "Shut up!" And then she fell on top of him, laughing too. Somewhile afterwards they had forgotten what they had been laughing about. The cushion that Maggie had dropped in the curry was wedged under their shoulders. They made love. It was good. The past and the future would demand attention soon. Not now. Just now all was at peace.

Out of the mass of information that came pouring into police headquarters there was one item that Maybridge looked at with quickening interest. A neighbour of the Webbers who lived opposite to the Brays worked on the hospital telephone exchange. The night that Sally Gray had been murdered he had driven home at twelve-thirty. Webber, he said, had arrived within minutes. He remembered this particularly because Webber accused him of blocking his garage entrance. He had moved his car so that Webber could get in. The information had been given to Stannard—not casually as one neighbour to another—but officially. Stannard had happened to be on duty and had received it and noted it down.

Maybridge called Stannard in and asked him what he made of it.

"Obviously," Louis pointed out, "Webber was lying about the time."

Maybridge parodied him. "Obviously. But why should—what's the man's name?—Stephenson think that it mattered a damn what time Webber got in?"

Louis said that there were rumours going around about Webber.

Maybridge had already guessed this. "And their source?"

"I don't know, sir. They certainly didn't originate with me."

"You're aware that our enquiries are strictly confidential?"

"Of course."

He risked the question he had thought of asking somewhile ago. "Stannard, you've been a neighbour of the Webbers for quite some time. What's your impression of the man? Could he have done it?"

Stannard replied softly, "You don't really want my opinion, sir. And in any case, I'd rather not answer."

Which, Maybridge knew, was answer enough. Rumours usually grew slowly; they didn't assume the nature of a forest fire. You stamped on them before they took hold, but before you could do that you had to find the source. If not Stannard—then who? He was the one who had access to information. He amended it. One of the many who had access. McKendrick was in with the Chief Constable. He had probably been told more than he should have been told. It would be heresy to say so, but he could think what he liked. And then there was the Gray girl—Sally's sister. In the early days she had buzzed around the police station and been a pestilential nuisance. Later the young constable who had her under surveillance had quit the Force— why?

In light of the new evidence he knew he would have to interrogate Webber again. And that would add more fuel to the fire. But if Webber were guilty then surely he deserved to be burnt. Was there an if? Some time ago he had told Rendcome that he had a feeling about Webber's guilt. He still had. But he wanted something solid to go on. An unshakable witness would do. A confession would do even better.

The second summons to the police station did not take George by surprise. He felt as if a lethal virus had entered his bloodstream and infected him with a type of emotional leukaemia. One of the symptoms of true leukaemia was fatigue. He felt a fatigue of the spirit—and of the flesh, too. He didn't want to fight. He felt too tired to bother. His colleagues were treating him with extreme politeness—or was it caution? There was no spontaneity any more. No jokes. No one told him about the rumours. They didn't have to. He could smell them—almost taste them. He wished he could vomit them out of his system. He wished he could go away—take Sue with him and go away. Mike was still with the Brays. As surrogate parents they were giving him a whale of a time. He sent cards home with his name scrawled on them and he had spoken to Sue a couple of times on the phone. They seemed to be living on chips and fish fingers and baked beans. He could swim—well, nearly. His nose was peeling with sunburn. Uncle Eric had bought him a red spade and Auntie Sylvia had bought the three of them kites. He didn't want to come home yet. He didn't have to did he? Not yet. The last bit of the conversation hadn't pleased Sue. "I'm glad he's happy, but do you suppose it's natural for a young child to be so contented away from home?" He had said sharply, "Yes— perfectly natural," and had gone on to say that under the circumstances—and then stopped. She had known what he meant. He had come across her reading the McKendrick article and she hadn't even commented on it, just put it quietly away. And so it was building up. Soon in the hospital the animosity would be overt. As long as the hurt didn't reach Sue he could stand it. On her own self-created little island of isolation she

129

should be all right. The Brays weren't there to carry tales, and wouldn't in any case. Tessa, staunch, loving but tactless, might let slip a careless word. She couldn't be warned. Nothing could be said. The illness had to run its course—and at the end of it . . . ?

Maybridge said quietly, "Try to bring your attention to bear on what I'm telling you. You could be in serious trouble. Think back. Be accurate. We have a witness who states you got home on Monday, the first of July—the night of Sally Gray's murder—at twelve-thirty, not eleven-fifteen."

"A neighbour? Stannard?" It didn't surprise him.

"No—not Stannard." He decided to divulge the source of his information. "Stephenson. He lives at number twelve."

"Oh." He was mildly surprised. He and Stephenson had had the occasional drink together. They had nothing in common, but as far as he was aware there had never been any animus. His wife collected for church jumble sales. Perhaps she hadn't liked Sue's last lot of cast-offs. Past caring about Maybridge's reaction, he told him about the jumble sale. "Not up-market enough. Church worker seeks revenge." It was bitterly jocular.

"For a man of considerable intelligence," Maybridge said crisply, "you're behaving with extreme stupidity. You're aware, I suppose, that you could be held here—for several hours if necessary—until you give us the information we want?"

"At this stage, do I ask for my lawyer?"

"No. But the way you answer my questions now will make it clear whether or not you'll need a lawyer in the future. Where were you on the night of Sally Gray's murder? What were you doing until twelve-thirty in the morning?" And don't tell me, he thought, that you were walking on the bloody Downs.

George leaned back in his chair and almost toppled it. He felt he wanted movement. He wanted to walk around the room. There was a cramp building up in his thigh. This eyeball to eyeball confrontation with Maybridge was like being held in a magnetic field. He wanted to break out of it.

He said roughly, "It's my word against Stephenson's. Why believe him?"

"Because we know exactly where he was on the night of the murder. The rehearsal you were attending finished at ten. You

130

didn't tell us that. We checked it. You said you got in at eleven-fifteen. Even if that were true there's still a time discrepancy. What were you doing between ten and eleven-fifteen?"

"I don't remember. I don't remember what I was doing a week ago—let alone several weeks ago. I suppose I told you in my statement what I was doing. Read it back to me."

"A few years ago," Maybridge said, "the penalty for murder was death by hanging. A verdict that concentrated the mind. I don't personally hark back to those days. I'm in the small minority that believes judicial murder to be obscene. On the other hand, the crime of murder is obscene—and in this case we're dealing with three. I don't like your levity. I don't understand it. Two young girls and one middle-aged woman have been brutally killed. They were gagged, raped and strangled. Was that the sequence, Mr. Webber? At what stage did you apply the gag—and when did you remove it?"

George's heart beats were slow and very heavy. The cramp in his thigh was unbearable. He thought of his own personal pain and not beyond it. When the cramp eased and his heart beats became normal he looked at Maybridge again.

"You're accusing me?"

"I'm asking you. And I want an answer."

"All right—here's your answer. I have never killed anybody. I have never maimed anybody. I have never, to my knowledge, hurt anybody. You won't, of course, take my word for it. So what do I do? Abase myself? Grovel? Or switch my mind off from something that's too crazy to contemplate?"

And that, Maybridge thought, could be just it. For most of the time you throw up mental blocks. Are you a psychopath who can switch your mind off the murder very soon after you've committed it? We've had those before. An act of savagery followed by a period of forgetfulness during which life goes on as normal. A psychopath can be gentle, too. A psychopath can be a loving husband—a kind neighbour—a good friend—for most of the time.

"I think it might be better," he replied quietly, "if you switched your mind on. I want you to write your statement again. You must think back to the rehearsal on the night of Sally Gray's murder—Monday, the first of July. The fact that it was a Monday might help—the first day of the working week.

131

Take the weekend as a whole. The last weekend of June. I'll leave you to get on with it. You might think better on your own. One of my constables will be outside the door. When you've finished, call him. I'll come back. You'll sign it in my presence." He put some sheets of paper and a pen on the table and stood up. "Take your time. There's no hurry."

George watched him go.

The room became normal again. The sun was shining in. One of the floor tiles was cracked. The electric clock lurched from minute to minute. It was twenty minutes to four.

'Once upon a time,' he wrote, 'on an evening a long time ago, my son, Mike, was playing ball in the garden with my wife, Sue. It was a big red ball—very soft—very bouncy. He threw it up into an apple tree. My wife, Sue, who was very agile, very quick, climbed up into the tree after the ball. It was at the far end of a branch and she couldn't quite reach it. So she went higher. But the branch that held the big red bouncy ball was a weak branch and when she put her weight on it, it snapped. Had she fallen on to the grass it would have been quite all right, but she fell on to a cast-iron wheelbarrow—on her back. And it wasn't all right. And it hasn't been all right since.'

And that, he thought, is my first false start. He crumpled it and threw it into the wastepaper basket.

And now for complete fabrication. Something very plausible.

'On the night of Monday, the first of July, I attended a rehearsal of *Otello*. It was a pleasant warm evening. The good weather may have been responsible for the fact that a lot of the opera company didn't turn up. We finished rather earlier than usual as the rehearsal wasn't going well. When I left—about ten—I had difficulty starting my car. The battery was flat. When I eventually got it going I took the longer route home—through the city centre. I arrived home at eleven-fifteen.

'My wife, who is an insomniac, said that she would like a run in the car, that it might help her to sleep. Earlier, she told me, there had been a particularly beautiful sunset through the beech trees at the bottom of the garden and she had an urge to get out into the country. Our son was safely asleep and we didn't intend leaving him for long. The July night was bright with stars and the air was clear and still warm. We drove—not to the

Downs, but to Claverham Woods. We both stayed in the car. Shortly after twelve we returned and I carried her in. I was unable to put my car in the garage as my neighbour, Stephenson, was badly parked too near the entrance. I could see by the light in his hall that he was up so I knocked on his door and asked him to move his car, which he did.'

He was about to sign it but remembered that Maybridge wanted to be present. He told the constable he was ready.

Maybridge returned almost immediately. It hadn't taken Webber long. He told him so and then took the statement and read it back to him. He kept his voice flat and expressionless as he did so. "Do you want to add anything or delete anything?"

"No."

"You're sure?"

"Quite."

"Then sign it and date it."

George did so. He wanted to yawn and had to clamp his jaws together to stop himself. He had fallen asleep on a beach once. Mike had covered his legs with sand. When he had awoken the waves were lapping his feet. Sue was at the far end of the beach queueing up to give Mike a donkey ride. He had told them aggrievedly that he might have drowned and Mike had laughed so much he had hiccups.

Maybridge was saying something. He forced himself to listen.

"You're not thinking of going away at any time in the near future?"

No. Nothing pleasant was scheduled to happen in the near future.

He said he wasn't.

"Good. And don't change your mind." He tapped the statement. "This won't be the end of it."

"It's surely sufficiently comprehensive to cover every point?"

Maybridge didn't answer, but saw him to the door. He didn't need to compare this second statement with the first, but nevertheless he did.

'On the night of the first July I spent the early part of the evening at home with my wife and son. The weather was inclement for the middle of summer, it was grey and showery.

133

My son went to bed at seven after I had given him a milk drink. I read him a story and then went downstairs and had coffee and sandwiches with my wife before leaving for a rehearsal of *Otello* at eight. After the rehearsal ended I drove home and arrived at eleven-fifteen.'

It was signed and dated the fifth of July.

He pinned the two statements together and then noticed the crumpled page in the wastepaper basket. He retrieved it and smoothed it out. 'Once upon a time . . .' He read on.

Detective Superintendent Claxby hadn't been impressed with the vendetta theory. Maybe this would impress him. Kick pity out. Concentrate on the murders not on the reason for them. He pinned the three pieces of paper together and took them through to the Superintendent. The Chief Constable was with him. He handed the papers to Rendcome first. Rendcome read them and passed them to Claxby. "It seems," he said, "we're getting somewhere. But we're not there yet."

Eighteen

"WHAT DO YOU SUGGEST I TELL THEM?" SUE ASKED. "That we don't know when we can go? They haven't seen Mike since this time last year. It's natural for grandparents to want to see their grandchild."

She had gone to the unexpected trouble of making pancakes. They were thick and leathery and even with a liberal sprinkling of sugar and plenty of lemon juice George found them difficult to eat.

He said that he wasn't due for leave.

"But you can arrange to take some early next month, perhaps? They're not rigid about that sort of thing."

Next month—perhaps. He didn't know. "I can't be definite."

"Is there any reason—apart from the hospital?"

He knew then that she was probing. Instead of asking the question directly she was throwing out feelers. After the night when she had tried to force herself in to some show of sexual feeling she hadn't spoken about it. He hadn't told her of his second interview at the police station and about Stephenson. Tessa might have told her. Anger against Tessa flared up and then died away. At least Tessa would have championed his cause. He could imagine her: "If they've been interrogating him, Sue, then they're moronic swine."

Moronic or not, the police seemed to have a case and were constructing it carefully brick by brick. When the bars were finally placed across the window, that would be it.

135

In the meantime Sue's parents wanted them to go there for a holiday.

He pushed the remaining pancakes away.

Normally, in a case like this, you told your wife to go on her own. But what was normal in a case like this?

She folded the letter and put it back in the envelope. "The holiday doesn't matter," she said. "Your reason for not being able to go does. The police have told you not to go, haven't they? That's what it's all about."

"Tessa?"

"No. But when you came in the other day I knew."

He supposed he should be grateful for that much rapport. This was the essence of loving a person. You share the same blood, almost.

He told her about Stephenson and the interview. "My statement squared it with them. There was a discrepancy in the timing. I told them we had been out for a drive to Claverham Woods and got in shortly after twelve."

Her face was very drawn and thin. "Which was a lie."

"A white one—a necessary one. This is a murder investigation, not an ecclesiastical examination."

"I'll support you, of course. If they ask. It's fortunate they haven't asked already. Which of the three murders are we talking about?"

"Sally Gray. On the first of July."

She was twisting the envelope over and over in her fingers. "And where were you until after twelve?"

"I don't know. I can't remember. After rehearsals I usually park the car somewhere quiet. Walk for a while. Music blurs reality: it takes time for the outside world to come back in again. That sounds stupid. I know what I mean. The police don't. They want details. An alibi." He took the envelope away from her. "Stop being so troubled about it."

"It doesn't occur to you, I suppose," she said, "that anything that happens to you happens to me. Anything you feel, I feel."

"It will pass. Everything will be all right eventually."

"Oh - yes," she said, "sing bright songs of Zion— encapsulate me in something impenetrable—shove me up on an altar. Why the hell don't you rant at me when I don't keep the

136

place clean? Why carry me about upstairs when there's a mobile chair there permanently for me to get myself around on? I'm your old man of the sea. I sit on your shoulders until you're bent double with the weight of me. You need a woman. Get one. Tell me. I don't care. I'll be glad for you. Heave me off your back. Lead a normal life. Ditch me, if you have to.''

He thought she was going to cry. Her face worked, but no tears came.

"I suppose,"he said, "that this is the point at which I tell you I haven't murdered anyone.''

She looked at him, appalled, and then the tears did come. He went over to her and tried to take her in his arms, but she pushed him away.

He had had to say it.

It had needed to be said.

God help us both, he thought. He began clearing the dishes and took them through to the kitchen. He could hear her muffled sobs and closed the door so that he couldn't hear them. He ran the two taps hard and then took one of the plates and hurled it against the back door. Pieces of blue china shattered on the coir doormat. One of the larger pieces stood sideways up against the door. He waited several minutes before getting the brush and pan. The mat smelt of dust.

When he returned to her they were both calm.

She held out her hands to him and he took them. She needed a handkerchief and he fetched her one from upstairs. A mobile chair upstairs—a mobile chair downstairs—a stair lift in between. She managed all day without him. Could she manage for more than a day, if it ever came to that? Could she manage for a lifetime?

The first anonymous letter arrived the following morning. It was a pale pink note let with forget-me-nots around the edges. The three words on it were written with a green ballpoint pen.

You Murdering Bastard.

He had picked it up with the rest of the mail and put it on the breakfast table. Sue, noticing the feminine-looking envelope, had assumed it was for her and had opened it.

She had been eating toast. She read the letter and couldn't swallow the piece in her mouth. She had had to take it out and cover it with her napkin. He couldn't understand why she should feel sick and then he read the letter and understood.

He didn't know what to say. He felt very cold. He didn't realise he was shivering.

She said almost primly, "I think I know how to kill. I think I could do it very easily."

The letter was open on the table between them. She picked up the butter knife in her fist and brought it down in a swift vicious movement so that it tore through the paper and tore the cloth under it.

"Oh dear," she said, in the same odd, little-girl voice. "We should have taken it to the police—and now we can't."

He didn't tell her that they couldn't anyway. He was beginning to be more concerned about her reaction to the letter than the letter itself. He couldn't go to work and leave her like this.

He took the letter and tore it up.

She watched him take out his lighter and burn the fragments in the grate. The last piece to burn was a bunch of forget-me-nots.

"A woman," she said. "Wouldn't you agree? Very feminine notepaper."

He agreed she might be right.

"Or a man," she went on, "trying to throw us off the scent. The printing looked masculine, wouldn't you say?"

He conceded that it was.

"Or a bloody bi-sexual lunatic." She, too, was trembling now. She felt sick in her mind. She wanted to scream.

He went into the hall and phoned the hospital. He told them he wouldn't be coming in. He said the first thing that came in to his head, "A throat virus—it will probably be clear by tomorrow."

She had heard him. "You're a very good liar."

"Yes, when necessary."

"What are we going to do?"

In the long term he didn't know. The present moment was his immediate concern. "I'm going to take you out somewhere—just for a few hours away from here."

It was a beautiful day. He thought of the Downs and he thought of Claverham Woods and rejected both as being too evocative. He thought, too, of visiting Mike, but neither of

138

them was sufficiently calm for that. They had taken a cottage once in the Mendips. It was a couple of hours' drive away. There was a spinny near it and a stream. They might gain a measure of calm there. He suggested it and she agreed. He cut sandwiches and put a flask of coffee in the picnic basket.

She remarked that they hadn't been for a drive on their own for a long time, "I can't think why, can you?"

He could, but didn't say. She never wanted to go anywhere.

It was after they had left the city environs that he suspected that they were being followed. The police car wasn't marked and the man driving it wasn't in uniform. The road to the hamlet was very minor and very narrow. The grey car, discreetly behind, followed the same route. He didn't mention it to Sue, but anger was tensing his muscles and she sensed it.

"What's the matter?"

"Nothing."

"*Tell* me."

"I think we're being tailed."

She looked through the rear window and couldn't see anything. "There's no other car around—just a tractor in the distance."

The fields were the soft green-gold of late summer. A grey road winding gently through fields of corn. And then she saw the grey car on the grey road.

"Stop and let him pass."

He drew up at the side of the road. The grey car, some way behind, stopped too.

She waited impatiently. "We could be mistaken."

"Yes," he said reassuringly. "Very likely."

The last time they had visited the cottage she had been able to walk. He had forgotten that there were three stiles along the river path. Each time they arrived at a stile he had to put her to sit at the side of the path while he lifted the chair over.

When they reached the spinny he was sweating with the effort.

He put her to sit in the shade of the trees and sat beside her. Clusters of vermilion poppies grew along the bank of the stream. Gnats hovered a few inches over the water. There was a smell of wood smoke and of burning stubble from a far-off field. Upon the hill the cottage, shuttered and empty, looked smaller and older than he remembered it, as if physically touched by time.

In the distance, on the far bank, a man strolled. He was city-suited but had taken off his jacket and rolled up his shirt sleeves. He didn't glance at them.

That's right, George thought viciously, be around. I might do away with my wife. I might, God help me, do away with you.

Sue asked to be taken out of her chair and put to sit on the grass. "Now, sit beside me—or, better still, lie," she said. "Put your head in my lap. We've come here for a bit of peace—and nobody—not that lout over there—nobody—is going to spoil it."

She seemed completely recovered now, he thought. Her voice was calm again. He did as she suggested and let her thighs cushion his head. He closed his eyes and the sun was red through the lids.

"Last time we were here," she reminded him gently, "you and Mike went fishing for stickleback—remember?" Her fingers were smoothing back his hair.

He played along with it. "And he fell in a cowpat on the way back to the cottage."

"Which wasn't funny at the time—but is now." I should follow that up with a philosophical remark about the appalling present and the certainty of a glorious future, she thought, but I can't.

The man had gone past the bend in the stream and was crossing the shallow part and coming on to their side of the bank. He was going up into the trees now and was somewhere in the shadows. She couldn't see him, but sensed he was still there.

They would have been better at home.

George would have been better at work.

But how were things at work?

Someone at work might have sent that letter.

He was asleep on her lap—or was he pretending to be asleep? No, he was asleep. She kept running her fingers through his hair. Could they make false accusations stick? Could they convict on circumstantial evidence? Why didn't he tell her where he had been when he returned late? Why could they communicate about everything, but not that? Just walking through the darkness? It was inconceivable. It had to be true.

When he awoke she told him that the man had gone. ''He was nothing to do with us. Shall we have the sandwiches now?''

He spread out the picnic on a blue tea towel and poured the coffee into yellow plastic cups. The cheese in the sandwiches was melting into the butter. Neither was hungry but they did their best to eat.

On the drive home the grey police car reappeared.

Neither mentioned it.

There were three more anonymous letters on pretty pastel paper. They all said the same thing. He intercepted them and tore them up.

The fourth came by a later post after he had gone to work. It was in a brown manilla envelope. The letters were cut out from a newspaper and stuck on to brown wrapping paper.

She read them, her armpits wet with sweat.

''You prowl the Downs by night like a predator. God sees you. I see you. You are a man of the night. A man of blood. Take me on your night prowls. Together we will kill—kill—kill. . .''

There was more. It was obscene. At the bottom of the page was a drawing—a crude piece of lavatory graffiti.

She backed away from it. It was untouchable. She wheeled herself into the kitchen and then out into the garden. She forced herself to breathe slowly. The garden was full of flowers and birdsong. The garden was clean. The sky was a wash of blue. She lay back in her chair and felt the breeze on her flesh. She hadn't prayed for years, she didn't know how to pray now. The word clean kept going through her mind—clean—clean—clean. . .

After half the morning had gone she wheeled herself back into the house. Using the fire tongs she picked up the letter and the envelope and put them in the grate. She didn't watch them burn, but when she turned her chair to the grate again they were ashes. She raked them through the firebars until nothing remained.

Still with a feeling of being contaminated she took the

stairlift and then the chair into the bathroom. She hadn't bathed on her own since the accident. It wasn't easy, but it was possible. She lay in the bath a long time. She wished she could wash her mind, too.

When George returned at shortly after five she was calm and welcoming. He guessed by the wet towels that she had bathed and accused her of taking unnecessary risks. "You might not have been able to get out. Next time if you want to bath wait until I'm in."

She told him not to sap her confidence. That it had been lovely. That she had managed terribly well.

He remembered her outburst about the old man of the sea. She was no burden. When you loved a person the word didn't apply. He began telling her, but she stopped him impatiently.

"Today," she said, "there was no letter."

He had been afraid to ask it.

That night she asked for sleeping tablets. "And try to get some sleep yourself. Don't bother to turn me—surely there's no need."

He knew that. In the beginning turning her had been a reassuring contact—a sharing of her weakness. "It's become such a habit, I do it in my sleep almost." He opened the bedroom window a little. "Too cold for you?"

"Just right."

He lay in his own bedroom thinking over the day. What was that about through a glass darkly? He seemed to see his colleagues through shaded lenses. Colleagues? A cosy word. It no longer applied. In the canteen today he had sat alone. The occasional glance had been like a swift rub of sandpaper before a mutual looking-away.

He wished he could take a sleeping pill himself, but was afraid he might sleep too deeply and not turn Sue. There were never to be any omissions—never any falling away. The aids were there, but were no substitute for his physical presence. The ceiling-mounted electric lift helped her in and out of bed when he wasn't around. A similar arrangement got her in and out of the bath, but only when he wasn't there—and he made a point of being there. The bath must have been slippery with soap. Had she fallen and struck her head . . .

He forced himself not to think of what might have happened.

She had coped. According to Tessa and the various assortment of social workers who had come and gone, she could cope a great deal better if she tried. But why try now?

He slept fitfully and awoke at three. It was time to turn her. The moon was bright and shining directly on her face. Her eyelids were flickering and then she began turning her head from side to side and moaning. She rarely had nightmares, but he could see she was having one now. The sleeping pills should have given her a deeper sleep. He spoke her name quietly.

"Sue?"

Suddenly she was struggling to sit up and then her eyes were open and she was looking at him.

He knew terror when he saw it and he was looking at it now.

"It's all right—it's a nightmare—you're safe—" he was babbling the words at her, not daring to go any nearer to her. "I'll get you water." He almost fell in his haste to get away from her. He couldn't bear the look in her eyes.

She was afraid of him.

He ran water into a tumbler, but his hands shook so much the water slopped over his feet. He waited several minutes before going back to the room and then he put the light on and went over to draw the curtain.

She way lying down again, her eyes closed, and she was breathing evenly—too evenly. He put the tumbler of water down on the bedside table. The last time she had had a nightmare—a long time ago—he had held her in his arms while she had told him about it. Afterwards he had lain beside her and held her for the rest of the night.

He left the room quietly and went back to his own. He had smoked three cigarettes in succession standing by his window and looking down into the moonwashed garden when she called him.

He went back to her and stood by her door. His mind in the last half hour had been empty of everything except the knowledge of pain.

She said quietly, "You left the light on. I could smell your cigarette. Can't you sleep?"

She didn't mention her dream.

He suggested she might like a drink of something . . . tea, perhaps? His voice was stiff, polite, as if they were strangers.

143

"No—not tea—not anything. Just company. Lie beside me."

"Is that what you want?"

The nightmare was still too near. For this sort of battle you needed strength. She thought she had it. She forced herself to have it.

"Yes, that's what I want."

It didn't ring true.

He told her gently that she would sleep better on her own. "A dream frightened you—it was just a dream."

He wondered if he dared kiss her. He wondered how he had appeared in her dream. He wondered how much of this he could bear. Why me, he thought, why me?

He said, "I love you." And she answered that she knew.

This time he put the light out when he left her and she lay in the darkness thinking about him.

I know, she thought, I know, I know, I know.

It was like a litany.

I love you.

I know.

Nineteen

JANINE FLEW OVER UNEXPECTEDLY FROM FRANCE AND WAS waiting for Paul in his consulting room when he had finished the day's operations. His mind was on the last case—the removal of a parasagittal meningioma. The benign tumour had been situated far forward compressing the frontal lobes and beginning to involve the motor cortex. The patient, a woman of fifty, had been seen by Ian Mavor as well as himself during the preoperative days. The personality changes due to the tumour had involved some pretty bizarre behaviour. Her hostility had been directed against red-haired customers at the shop where she worked. Her weapon, a pair of scissors, had fortunately only inflicted minor wounds. Removal of the tumour restored her to a normal mental state and prevented the progressive paralysis which would have followed in time. Very satisfying. Not particularly difficult surgery. Interesting teaching material. Ian had assisted capably and had seemed totally absorbed. There was nothing better than the removal of a mind-blasting tumour to give young neurosurgeons a strong sense of vocation. A little drama went a long way. He went into his consulting room, smiling.

"Janine!" Astonished, he went over and kissed her. "You didn't tell me you were coming."

She had noticed the smile and felt a touch of relief. She had come on impulse—perhaps unnecessarily. She told him that she had seen a copy of his interview with the Press.

"Oh, that—by God!"

She understood his embarrassment. It was just as well he hadn't read the French version. The English expression 'sob story' occurred to her. He would have given it neat—like a good Cognac. The Press had added saccharine—and so what of it? The public slurped happily and they depended on the public for results. She asked if there had been any.

"There hasn't been an arrest yet." He hesitated. "Rumours—perhaps unfounded."

She demanded to be told them. It was with some unease that he complied.

"And Rendcome has had him grilled?"

A vision of burning flesh came to him. She had made it sound that way. Janine, like many otherwise gentle people, was of the flog 'em and hang 'em brigade. That he could easily kill Maggie's killer he didn't deny. In the days of quietly contained rage following her murder he had fantasised about personal retribution. When he had found Harriet dead he had believed himself over the edge of sanity and in the dark lands of uncontrollable emotion. By the time the name and face of Webber began to emerge he had attained a degree of calm. No one knew yet. It was possible. It was yet to be proved. There were times, particularly when he was tired, when he felt he was over the edge again and hatred took control. Proof was unimportant then. To hell with pussy-footing. Charge him. Or let me get my hands on him.

Him?

Webber?

Perhaps.

But 'perhaps' wasn't good enough.

For his own sake, as well as Janine's, he had to hold his feelings in check.

"I'm not in Rendcome's confidence. He says he's following up every lead he gets, and I've no doubt he is."

He sat down and consciously relaxed his muscles. She was watching him keenly and recognised his physical reaction to a long period of concentration in the theatre.

"Paul . . . I was very sorry to hear about Harriet."

He hadn't known that she was aware of the relationship. "So you knew?"

146

"Of course. And I was pleased. You needed someone. Why didn't you marry her?"

It was a question he had been asking himself. They would have married eventually if . . .

This was too raw to be spoken about. He made a dismissive gesture with his hands and she understood.

"All right—I'll say nothing more. But Maggie . . ." Her eyes were tearless. They had both stepped onwards from that sort of facile emotional relief, but her feelings were his feelings, and in this they understood each other and were in complete accord.

He told her simply and truthfully that he was glad she had come. They could only share this with each other. Others were kind. Others listened. But only they—the two of them—knew.

She planned to stay a couple of days only. "Claude's gone to Boulogne—a business deal. He rarely leaves me on my own. He is considerate. The marriage is good. But I, on my own, thought of you on your own . . . as things are now. I had to come."

He was touched that she should worry about him. "I'm all right. Managing."

"With Maggie you were more than managing. She was good for you. She was always more your child than mine. The father-daughter relationship is very special. I was selfish, perhaps, that I tied her so close to me."

It was a criticism that he tended to agree with, but it wasn't the time to say so. Instead he told her about Ian Mavor. "He's a likeable lad with a promising future. They were lovers, I think. It took me some while to get used to that idea. Now I accept it." He went on to tell her about Ian's friendship with Rachel Gray. "She's as packed full of hatred as explosives in a bomb. I think the Webber rumours started there."

"Then here's to Rachel Gray and may he explode in hell."

"Now—hold on—no one knows."

"Then it's time they did. What is Rendcome doing? Is he a friend or isn't he? Why doesn't he tell you everything? He will tell me everything."

He tried to dissuade her from seeing Rendcome at his home that same evening, but she wouldn't be dissuaded. He went with her with some reluctance.

Rendcome, surprised, annoyed, coolly civil, heard her out.

"Charge him," she said, "convict him. It is unfortunate that this is not France. In France we have the guillotine."

She read his expression. "No, Nigel, I am not civilised. I am not forgiving. Not humane. But I am one good positive thing—I am Maggie's mother."

That was unanswerable.

His anger abated.

He didn't like her. He never had. But he understood her and he understood Paul. It would be the greatest mistake of their lives if the death of Maggie drew them together again on a permanent basis. Sharing grief might help the healing process, but personalities remained the same. Paul would find solace somewhere some day, if not with another Harriet then with his work. He was a survivor. It was the Webbers of this world who drifted into disaster—or actively sought it. He still wasn't sure. The young couple who had come in today to report sighting a man in the vicinity of Harriet's garden on the night of the murder were either bona fide or, like most of the others, out for grabs. The two thousand pounds' reward would make a nice down-payment on their mortgage. According to Maybridge their timing of the sighting had been about right and the man they saw had been carrying something that could have been a violin case. Not *was*. *Could have been*. They thought they could identify him. Their description was woolly, but it could be Webber. The identity parade might clinch it. It was to be arranged for the following afternoon at five.

"I only wish," Janine was saying, "that you would *do* something."

He suggested pleasantly that he should pour them all a drink.

Obeying Maybridge's instructions George wore his dark suit for work and carried a lightweight macintosh. The temperature was up in the seventies and Sue had looked at him in astonishment. He was taking the mac to be cleaned, he told her, but couldn't think of an explanation about the suit. "Wear what you wore the night of the concert," Maybridge had said. "The mac, fortunately, is ubiquitous. There'll be a line-up of men of around your height and build wearing the same sort of clothes." He had gone on to explain about the couple. "They were walking their dog on the Downs. There's a cinder track running along the back of the houses which front on Beeches Close—where Doctor Brand lived. They saw someone answering your description walking near the track. The identity parade will eliminate you or . . ." He shrugged.

Dignity, George mused, self-esteem. At one time Maybridge would have approached me with civility. When was the 'Mr.' dropped? Now it's Do this, Webber—Do that, Webber—Get lined up with a lot of other sods. (Where did they get them from? Ex-cons? Policemen?—who?)

He had tried to kick back. "A couple of rapacious newlyweds want to put their greedy fingers on McKendrick's money—and you're asking me to oblige them. Why the hell should I?"

"To clear yourself." It was suave. "If you know yourself to be innocent an identity parade shouldn't worry you."

"Innocence—or guilt—has nothing to do with it. A person seen for a few minutes only in the dark just doesn't register in the memory."

"In that case you go home rejoicing."

"And if it goes the other way, as I'm sure you hope it will, and I'm mistakenly identified. What happens then?"

"Then, Webber, you start worrying. You get your lawyer."

"You take me into custody on suspicion of murder?"

"That about sums it up—yes."

And Sue? George thought. What about Sue? I suppose you send in your valiant team of social workers. Christ Almighty—who *tells* her?

He hadn't known what to do just before taking his leave of her. It was the line of least resistance to tell her nothing. He had tried forming sentences in his mind. "I'm dressed like this on police orders. I've been ordered to attend an identity parade. It's nonsense, of course, but I have to go. There's always a possibility that I might not come back. You might have to pack a suitcase for me. If you do you'll find some new underpants in the top drawer of my dressing-table. There are some socks there, too, without holes in them. You mustn't mind too much about any of it. They can't make anything stick. But they'll try. You'll have to make up a story for Mike. I've gone away on a course—or something. They probably won't allow bail. I don't

149

know how long a trial takes to prepare. They've got nothing to go on. They might even drop it. But if they don't . . . You're not to get into the bath on your own again. Let Tessa or the district nurse help. You should let someone come in and sleep at night. Perhaps the social services can arrange it.''

She had cut across his thoughts. ''What's the matter?''

He had nearly told her then, but the words were too brutal to get out. Too near the bone. A few weeks ago he would have been sure of her reaction: amazement—fury. She would have held him in her arms and trembled with rage. Now?

After the nightmare he hadn't been sure. She was trying too hard, and hating herself for having to try.

He told her coolly that nothing was the matter. ''I might be a little late home. I'll phone you if it's later than I expect.'' (Surely they would allow that?)

His kiss was perfunctory. Afraid of his own emotions he had been almost brusque. ''Have a good day—take care.''

As always he stopped before getting into the car and waved. She had wheeled her chair into the hall, as always, and waved from the open door.

Her smile was stiff with foreboding. What is it, she wondered? What is so different about today? What is happening? Why won't you tell me what's happening?

In a flurry of activity aimed mainly to deaden thought rather than to achieve a tidy house she moved around in her chair dusting and clearing. He had put a couple of chicken wings in a slow casserole whilst preparing the breakfast and she added herbs and peeled some potatoes. It was eleven o'clock when she heard the key in the lock and thought he had come back and then she heard her mother's voice. ''Sue? Darling! Surprise, surprise!''

Her mother smelt of jasmine. Her eyelids were too blue. She was slim, neat, cheerful. Never fussed. She was a rock of common sense in a turbid sea. Sue, in a sudden thankful regression to childhood, lifted her face to be kissed. She felt six years of age. Safe. Mummy was here—and Daddy, too. For a full five minutes she rejoiced as she had never rejoiced before.

Her parents exchanged glances over her head. Surprised. Pleased. The house, they noticed, shone with loving care. There was a good smell of cooking in the kitchen. Their maimed, awkward, lazy, beautiful and well-loved daughter was coping. She was coming to terms with her disability.

They asked her about Mike.

She reminded them that he was on holiday with the neighbours.

Her mother made coffee for the three of them. "Still?" When George was there she was always careful to leave the kitchen to him. He had insisted on the domestic role, unwisely she believed, but she had tactfully not interfered. It was on his insistence that she had the extra doorkey.

"Yes," Sue said, a trifle defensively, "still. He's enjoying it."

They had come down, her father told her, mainly to see her, of course, but also to run in the new car. He wheeled her over to the window and showed her the maroon hatchback with pride. There was plenty of room in the back for her chair, he said, and it wouldn't take them all that long to drive to West Bay. How about it? They had brought some skittles for Mike and he'd like to show him how to play. Eh? Good idea? Yes?

It had to be yes.

In their company she thought she could cope with Mike. He would be too delighted with his grandparents to look inside her mind with that penetrating look of his and ask her if she was hunky-dory. She couldn't think where he had learnt the expression and wished he would unlearn it. She had first heard him ask it of a shell-less snail in the garden.

Her mother, now that the first euphoria was over, asked it too.

"Everything going along well?"

"Fine!"

"George all right?"

"Yes—quite."

"It's a pity he can't be with us, but I'm sure he'll be glad we're taking you out on this lovely day. Will you phone him at the hospital—or write a note?"

It was easier to write a note. She wheeled herself over to the bureau and found paper and a ballpoint. Even the bureau was tidy: envelopes neatly stacked, pens and pencils in a box.

"Gone with parents to see Mike," she wrote. "Will be back this evening about . . . ." She looked enquiringly at her father.

"What time will we be home?" He told her around ten. She wrote "ten thirty to eleven" in case he worried. "Love Sue," she ended it and added kisses.

She propped the note up by the clock on the mantelpiece.

"And now," said her father, swinging her up into his arms, "I'll take you upstairs. First call the bathroom—call of nature—then out to the car while your mother sees that all is well and safe in the kitchen—eh?—yes?"

She had a sudden urge to be put down. It was too cosy. Unnatural. I'm a thirty-one-year-old woman and you're nearly sixty. I'm not your little girl. But more than anything I want to be—your little girl, running . . .

Running . . . Running . . .

Her father couldn't see her expression, but her mother could. "Sue, is anything worrying you?"

"Worrying me? No, of course not."

Only, George went out this morning and I've a terrible fear I'll never see him again.

Twenty

THE ONLY WAY TO COPE WAS TO SWITCH OFF. THIS WAS A modern day opera in modern dress. Setting: Out of doors in the yard of a police station on a very hot day. Even the tarmac was melting. What sort of music would suit this? A funeral march as the men assembled? No, they were walking too fast. No dignity. Everyone looked extremely embarrassed. A bevy of men in macintoshes looking damned silly. Nobody looked at anybody else.

Maybridge said, with a touch of sympathy, "It's a bit of an ordeal, I know. Stand wherever you want to."

It was easier to stand at the end. It might be better to stand in the middle, but to stand in the middle he would have to elbow his way in between the bloke with ginger hair and the one who kept fingering the boil on his neck. They were talking together and seemed to be buddies. He went to stand at the end. None of these men looked like him. The only things that looked alike were the macintoshes. He remembered buying his six years ago. He had worn it to the nursing home when Mike was born. Some pollen from the bunch of flowers he had been carrying had rubbed off on the sleeve. The pollen had made Sue sneeze and once started she couldn't stop. The mother in the next bed had said something scathing about spreading germs to the poor little ones and he and Sue had started to laugh.

He wanted to laugh now, which was quite ridiculous.

It was bubbling up inside of him. And so was a tune. *Peter and the Wolf*. They had walked on stage to a slowed-down version of that.

Certainly not a death march.

The man next to him had a Byronic profile spoilt by a tic in his left eyelid. Byron—born George Gordon Noel. Odd how irrelevant facts stuck in the mind. Well, they'd picked out someone who shared the same Christian name with him. Otherwise there was no resemblance at all. Byron in Greece. *Zoë mou, sas agapo*. My life, I love you. From what? 'Maid of Athens'? 'By love's alternate joy and woe, *Zoë mou, sas agapo . . .*'

Byron with a nervous tic.

What did he have to be nervous about? No one was going to point an accusing finger at him.

Got the beat of the poem in my head.

> 'Maid of Athens! I am gone:
> Think of me, sweet! when alone.
> Though I fly to Istambol . . .' (Istambol? Yes, Istambol.)
> 'Athens holds my heart and soul:
> Can I cease to love thee? No!
> *Zoë mou, sas agapo.*'

They were coming out now. Good God, they even had a dog with them! A cairn terrier with a red collar. The girl was blonde with a frizzed perm. Two of her front teeth stuck out. She wore sunglasses with pink frames. Her dress was a geometric pattern of blobs and circles—navy blue on white. Her sandals were white and scuffed. The man—her husband?—looked about seventeen. There were a few wispy hairs on his chin. You'll have a job to grow a beard, lad. Try again in five years' time when you've stopped growing. Your trousers are too short and you've got midge bites on your ankles.

Maybridge and another officer were saying something to them. They nodded and looked apprehensively at the line-up of men.

Don't be afraid of me, children. When you put your hand on my shoulder, or whatever it is you do, I promise I won't bite you. Or knee you in the stomach, or lay you flat and jump on you. I will submit. *Mea culpa*. Lead me to the gallows.

None of this is true.

God Almighty—it can't be.

It's a charade. A game set up by Stannard. Tessa's been too much around—is that it, Louis? Your precious Saint Theresa too caring, is that it? Well, she hasn't been around the last couple of days. Got her on a ball and chain?

They're coming up close now. They could have had the decency not to eat garlic—and on such a hot day. The dog is sniffing around my shoes. Try a little lick, boy. You might lick off the evidence. It's a wonder they didn't collect my shoes along with my violin. What are they doing with my violin all this time? Perhaps they'll give it back when they put me inside. Prison is supposed to be civilised these days. Let us all play jolly tunes together—a rhapsody for rapists—a mazurka for murderers . . .

The mascara on your pale blonde lashes is standing out like a row of little beads on yellow stalks. That's right. Look—look hard. What do I do—? Smile at you? Tell you I hope you'll have a lovely time with all that lolly?

And you—boy child—masquerading as a husband—did you get yourself in so deep with that little semi that you had to dream up something this outrageous to pay for it?

That's right—boy. You look hard, too. Like playing bingo, isn't it? Except that here the numbers aren't given to you—you have to choose . . . or do you?

They're moving on.

Well, of course.

Being fair.

Down the line—one, two, three—stop, look. That's the bloke with the boil. He's dabbing it with his handkerchief. He's as cool as if he's in his bathroom at home—completely indifferent to them.

They're going on again. Slowly. Right down to the end of the line.

And now they're coming back.

Sue, what am I going to tell you?

Why should one person mean so much to another person? Seven years ago I didn't know you existed. I slept—ate—breathed. Life was very easy—very low key.

I never meant to do this to you.

I'm your strength.

You need me. (Still? Please!)

I need you. (Very simply—very profoundly.)

The dog is at my shoes again. I'm tired. There's a small trickle of sweat going down my spine. I wish you'd get it over with, the two of you. Maybridge has told you, hasn't he? The one at the end. But don't hurry it. It looks bad if you do. Take your time.

She has scagged finger nails. She'll be the one to put her hand on me. Not him. He trails behind. Timid little boy husband with the large Adam's apple and the shifty eyes. One day, lad, you might have a son, too.

I mustn't think of Mike.

God damn you, get on with it!

So they don't put their hand on . . . they don't touch . . . they just go over and tell Maybridge without looking at me. Now they're going in with one of the other officers—click—click—little scuffed heels—one dirty deed on a lovely summer's day.

The men around him began to disperse and Maybridge came over. His face was expressionless. "Well—that's it."

Webber felt his body sag as the tension eased. "What do you mean?"

"You have just seen two upright young citizens who are so afraid of making the wrong choice that they haven't made any. As I told you earlier, you can go home rejoicing." He didn't add, "For the time being", but it was there in his expression.

George felt tears burning the back of his eyes and he blinked them away. He badly needed to go to the lavatory, but was determined to hold it until he got to the public lavatory in the town centre. After that he would go to a florist—or no, perhaps not. Let the day seem as normal as possible. Put the mac in the cleaners. He said he was going to do that, so better do it.

And then home.

Sue.

When he drove up to the Romney Hill estate at six-fifteen he was humming under his breath. No paradise, this, just a slice of neat suburbia, but particularly welcoming at this particular moment. There were kids on tricycles. One or two neighbours out in their gardens snipping lazily at overblown roses. Dead roses looked more sick than any other flower. Petals bursting into maturity and then falling away one by one. Had he changed his mind and got Sue a bouquet he would have gone in for something cool and white. Virginal. Sue, as she had become. Was it reaction to stress that made him feel sexually aware? Sue—I have been given a reprieve—we have more hours together—more days. Sleep with me.

He decided not to garage the car. It was a pleasant evening. They would perhaps have a drive together.

The neighbours in the immediate vicinity were as still as gargoyles on a church wall. He affronted them with a greeting. Whether they responded or not he didn't know. It was at that stage that he saw the broken window.

The tune died away from his mind and anger crept in. Careless kids with their damned balls. It would happen when Sue was on her own.

He let himself into the hall calling her name. No answer. She was in the garden, perhaps, sun-bathing? He looked there first after glancing casually into the living room. And then he went upstairs. She wasn't in the house. He went into the living room and his feet crunched on glass. The brick had landed on the polished mahogany table—polished? There was a piece of paper around it held with an elastic band.

Thick black letters on brown wrapping paper.

MURDERER.

His blood was humming in his ears.

A breeze was blowing in through the smashed window and touching the hairs on the back of his neck like small enquiring fingers. A bill for newspapers that had lived on the mantelpiece for days had blown on to the coal scuttle. Sue's note blown by the same capricious breeze was under the bookcase and out of sight.

It occurred to him with sudden terror that she had been hurt. The brick had struck her. She was at this moment in hospital. He walked very carefully into the hall and dialled the hospital. His fingers seemed too big. They kept missing the right numbers. He kept misdialling. When he got the number his voice was too choked at first to get out the query. And then he asked it, and began to tremble as he waited for the answer.

It was brisk, reassuring, and in the negative.

And so what . . . ?

He tried to get inside her skin and imagine what she would do. Her chair wasn't there. She had taken the chair and gone out. To Tessa, perhaps. He went across the road to the Stannards and rang the bell. There was no answer.

Panic pushed the last vestiges of clear thinking out of his mind. She was out somewhere in her chair—out in the bloody street on her own. He began running down Romney Avenue and into Romney Road. Kids playing hopscotch. Blue plastic bucket near a parked car. Smell of paint. Sticky green fence. A car horn, too close, blaring at him. No sign of her anywhere. Back to the house then—and what?

One of the gargoyles was deigning to speak to him. Even daring to touch him. A hand on his arm.

He identified her as Mrs. Parcival, a neighbour of the Stephensons.

She was saying something about Sue having gone out with her parents. Ridiculous—her parents weren't there. Her parents lived in Worcestershire in a former manse with green fields around it.

She was insisting. "I saw them arrive and I saw them go. Mrs. Webber's father was carrying her. They put the wheelchair in the boot and then they went off."

She looked beyond him at the broken window.

"Had I seen that happen I would have reported it to the police. Every man is innocent until he is proved guilty. England has become a land of hooligans."

He thanked her politely and agreed.

Duty done, she removed her hand from his contaminating arm and returned to her own front garden.

He went back to his house and sat in the living room for several minutes without moving.

Mrs. Parcival would have phoned the police.

Sue wouldn't, for obvious reasons, phone the police.

Sue phoned her parents.

She hadn't phoned him.

She had sat in the debris for as long as it took her parents to drive over and then she had gone with them.

He didn't blame her.

He wasn't even surprised.

Total silence was a concept that he was beginning to understand. She hadn't known what to say so she had said nothing. In time there would be communications. Awkward words on a telephone. A meeting eventually, with her parents to escort her. Her father had never liked the marriage. 'A purposeless young man' had been his summing up at the time, 'frittering away his ability when he could be channelling it for your mutual good'. Afterwards he had accepted the inevitable and covered his dislike with a brisk heartiness.

They would look after her very well.

They would look after Mike, too.

His son.

Everything that gave meaning to his life had been taken from him.

He had cigarettes in his pocket but he couldn't find his lighter. He went into the kitchen for matches and smelt the chicken casserole. It was a pity to waste it. Hunger and the usual bodily functions went on. He ate some of it directly from the pot but discovered he wasn't hungry after all. He had come for matches. He went back to the living room and lit his cigarette. A splinter of glass stuck up dangerously from the hearth-rug and he picked it up and took it out to the bin.

He had smoked several cigarettes and was brushing up the remainder of the glass when he saw Tessa going past the side window to the back garden.

She let herself in through the open back door.

She wasn't surprised at what she saw. Mrs. Parcival had told her. She, in turn, had told Mrs. Parcival a lot of things. Her Irish temper, normally dormant, had been fuelled by outrage. May the whole street—the estate—the town—be condemned to everlasting damnation, she had shouted. Steven was stoned, she said, Peter crucified upside down, and look what they had done to the Blessed Lord.

Mrs. Parcival had called her an hysterical Catholic bitch. The fact that she might have said heretical—which she had confused with blasphemous—had stopped her in midsentence. Maybe her defence of George had gone a mite too far.

She crouched down beside him and took away the brush and pan. "Let me."

He went and sat again.

She brushed up all the glass and then she vacuumed the carpet. In ten minutes she had dusted all the surfaces of the furniture. Pieces of glass, as small as sugar crystals, got under her nails. She scrubbed her hands in the kitchen sink.

When she returned to the living room she asked him what he had done with it.

"Done with what?"

"Whatever they threw."

"A brick. It's by the bin."

She went out and saw it. He had made a half-hearted attempt to rip the paper off but most of it remained. She pulled away the elastic band and tore the paper into shreds.

So Sue couldn't take it.

Well, she could take it.

Her rage was abating in action, but it was still strong enough to quench tears. Now wasn't the time to cry. He had had enough of helpless women draining the blood out of him.

She went to look in the garden shed to see if there was any corrugated cardboard to nail across the window. There wasn't. She thought there might be some in her own shed and told him she was going across the road for a minute or two. "I need something thick enough and wide enough to cover the smashed glass."

He seemed barely aware of what she was doing.

She returned in about twenty minutes with a couple of pieces of cardboard and with his violin case. Her eyes were bright spots of anger. The violin case had been in an old tea chest wrapped in spider-infested sacking. Obviously Louis had been entrusted to return it and obviously he had maliciously hung on to it. The fact that his story about the forensic tests was true—and that George's version about lending it to a friend wasn't—had shaken her slightly. But if they had found anything incriminating—which they wouldn't—the violin case wouldn't have been entrusted to Louis to return.

She took it through to the living room and up-ended it by the piano. "It was in our shed. For goodness knows how long. I apologise for my bloody-minded husband."

Her anger surprised him a little. Did anything matter that much? He watched as she cut the cardboard to size and hammered it to the window-frame. He felt like an invalid put to sit

160

in a chair after a period in bed. Other people did things. Other people got on with it. The cardboard looked hideous and darkened the room. She drew the curtain across it.

"And now," she said, "I'll get you a cup of tea. Or would you rather have whisky?"

Tea, he said, would be fine. "Thanks very much."

They sat drinking it, on the surface companionably. Like a married couple, she thought, on an ordinary day. You have come home from work. The window has been broken—for ordinary reasons. We have been angry about it and now we are angry no more. Everything is smooth—easy—ordinary—because I have made it that way. With me there is no stress. You don't have to carry me around. I have an ordinary body with legs that move.

He wondered what he should say to her. You couldn't just sit for minutes on end and say nothing. But there was nothing to say. The photograph of Sue and Mike and himself was directly in his line of vision. He kept on looking at it without taking it in.

Tessa noticed and wondered if she dared remove it. Not yet. Perhaps later.

The future would be a golden time—sweet as a field of Irish corn. They wouldn't stay here. She would persuade him back to Ireland with her. The hospital environment was wrong—for both of them. A place capable of breeding the sort of rumours she had heard needed disinfecting. She had made untold enemies in the last week or so. Enemies who smiled derisively, sometimes politely, sometimes even kindly. But how can you be so sure, they had said, how can you possibly know?

Because my body tells me.

Because it told me a long time before my mind told me.

Because it is telling me now—and this time there is no restraint. No helpless, loving Sue, of the knowing eyes and the clever tongue.

Nothing. Just the two of us and silence.

He wasn't aware that she had left the room and gone upstairs. She had been calling for some time before he heard her. He wondered what she wanted and wished she would go home. She had been kind and practical and now her task was done.

161

She had chosen his bedroom. It faced the back, and the evening sky splashed the bed with carmine. He looked down at her dispassionately, feeling nothing, not even surprise. Her body was smaller than Sue's. Her nipples had pink aureoles, Sue's were brown. There was a faint line of an appendix scar running up from her groin. Sue's scar had been along the spinal cord. A useless cutting of flesh that had achieved nothing. McKendrick's voice came to him clearly. "I'm very sorry, old chap. I didn't hold out any promises, as you know. The injury is quite severe. She'll learn to live with it, in time, with your help."

Oh yes, McKendrick, old chap, she'll learn to live with it. Better than I shall learn to live with it. You should have had us on the operating table side by side—destroyed us both sexually at the same time—old chap.

She took his hand and pressed it hard against her mouth. He could feel her teeth—her tongue.

In a polite and slightly embarrassed acknowledgement he touched her coppery curls with his free hand. Sue's hair had been like a velvet curtain—thick, black, strong. He had tasted her hair, run it through his teeth, wrapped it around his wrists. Had McKendrick's love-play included playing with Harriet's hair? Were her limbs as rich as Sue's—old chap?

Anger began growing in him, melting his numbness, touching him with fire so that his flesh knew pain. This wasn't Sue. This was a pale, sweet, sex object, good, well-intentioned, nice. This was Tessa. He wanted to hurt her—even kill her. His fingers fluttered across her throat and then down to her breasts, her small pointed breasts. Sue's were round, full, warm. This was a creature of another breed—small, angular, body smelling of verbena.

He accepted what she had to give him. He accepted it savagely and with no tenderness.

She had expected a gentle loving—not this. Terrified, drowning in a maelstrom of sexual ecstasy, she at last pushed him away from her.

He was sweating and trembling when he got up from the bed and stood looking down at her. She was lying on her stomach now—weeping with pleasure.

162

He knew what he had to do.

In a red haze of anger he plotted the rest of the night's work.

The time of weakness—of grovelling acceptance—was over. He told her to get up.

Twenty-one

THE FACT THAT WEBBER HAD CONTACTED THE HOSPITAL IN an attempt to discover the whereabouts of his wife was common knowledge by early evening.

Rachel, going back to the flat for a couple of hours, met Ian on his way to the hospital. She told him what she had heard. "I had it from casualty. If she's left him, it's a bid for survival. If it's a cover-up on his part, then it's too late."

"Cover-up?"

"If she's found dead, then his reporting her missing would seem to put him in the clear." She was upset. She liked Sue. She wished Ian would say something comforting.

He was in no physical state to be comforting. "What's Webber afraid of—that she's had an accident?"

"That bastard isn't afraid of anything—only his neck. Not even that these days." She looked at him closely. "What's the matter?"

"Nothing."

Oh God, she thought, gloom and despondency. His mood had started building up at breakfast after he had risen early to do some studying.

"Your exams," she said crisply, "don't really matter a damn, you know. People do."

"Meaning Maggie?"

She hadn't been thinking of Maggie. She hoped that recently he hadn't been thinking about Maggie—too much.

She took his arm. "Come back to the flat. You don't have to be at the hospital yet."

He wanted to check up on some X-rays and go through some case histories. After that he would take a walk. Anywhere. On his own. He felt hot and rather sick.

Last night he had dreamt about Maggie. An odd, uneasy dream that made no sense.

He suggested that Rachel should cook a meal for herself. "I'll see you in the flat later. Don't bother cooking for me."

"What are you going to do now?"

"Make notes on a couple of case histories. See some X-rays."

Rachel remembered the subject matter of the text books he had left in an untidy pile on the kitchen table. She didn't have to be particularly astute to know what was wrong. "It's an occupational hazard," she said dryly, "to imagine that you're suffering from a parasagittal meningioma when all you've got is a hang-over." She grinned at him. "Too much beer, wouldn't you say? Or a personality change due to good old Scotch."

He wasn't smiling.

Occupational hazard—maybe. He had suffered in imagination from various diseases since starting the job. Fear of this particular disease tended to come and go. Since that operation with McKendrick he had brooded about it a lot. Even talked about it to Rachel. How much of her lunatic behaviour had the patient been aware of? How much had she remembered afterwards? He felt a sudden revulsion at the thought of the X-rays. He had a throbbing headache and it was getting worse. Headaches were symptomatic. It would be better to see the X-rays when his head was clearer and he felt calmer. And that went for the case histories, too.

"Ian, come back with me. This is your free time. I'm your case history. Study me."

"I'll come back later." He removed her hand from his arm.

He had a strong urge to walk the fields of his childhood. There had been the smell of gorse there, not the stink of diesel. The nearest he could get to clear fresh air here was on the Downs. A brisk walk might clear his head.

Without looking where he was going he took a step off the

165

pavement and a small grey car had to take swift avoiding action.

Rachel, annoyed, watched him go. He wasn't crossing the road with reasonable care. And he wasn't making for the hospital. The driver of the car had sworn at him—justifiably. There were times when she felt like swearing at him, too, and frequently did.

Frowning, she waited until he had arrived safely at the far pavement. He wasn't really sick, was he? He was just mildly obsessional. Most doctors were slightly paranoid at pre-examination times, weren't they? He wasn't all that odd.

Police Constable Naylor, the driver of the grey car, arrived at Romney Avenue nearly five minutes late for duty. When a git nearly flings himself under your wheels you tend to drive afterwards with the caution of an octogenarian. He took over from his colleague at the road junction where Webber's house could be observed. There had been nothing to report. He settled back with a cigarette.

Boredom and the thundery evening air made him sleepy and he almost missed the red Mini as it pulled out into Romney Road. Belatedly he recognised it as belonging to Stannard's wife. Webber was driving. She was sitting next to him. Webber's dark blue Vauxhall, details of which he knew extremely well, remained at the kerbside. He hastily memorised the Mini's number-plate and put a call through to Maybridge.

Maybridge, not surprised, gave him the necessary instructions and then contacted Stannard at the incident room.

"It seems," he told him over the phone, "that Webber is taking an evening jaunt in your wife's car. His reasons may be perfectly innocent—something wrong with his own car, perhaps. Naylor is following at a tactful distance and will keep reporting over the R.T. Your wife," he added, in a throwaway line like the flick of a whip-lash, "is in the car—but not driving. Is this something you want to handle yourself?"

The answer, he knew, was a foregone conclusion.

The fact that he might be igniting a potential time-bomb didn't worry him. He went on suavely, "He's not making for West Bay where his lad is. At the moment he's on the A46 heading north. Use one of the patrol cars and you'll be guided along the right route. Don't make a big drama of it—no sirens—

166

just find out where he's going—and why." He added politely, "Sorry Mrs. Stannard's got herself involved—quite innocently, I'm sure."

He wished he could see Stannard's face. The junior officer's clipped acknowledgement told him nothing.

It would be a pity, Maybridge thought as he hurried down to his own car, if this turned out to be a nice neighbourly little jaunt lasting an hour or so. But he had a gut feeling that it wasn't. Tonight there would be action. He had met Tessa Stannard a couple of times at police social functions—a pleasant, innocuous youngster, as naïve as they came. She was like a forest creature wandering through lion country. He wondered if she were accompanying Webber of her own free will.

Stannard had no doubt whatsoever about the matter. For obvious reasons Webber hadn't used his own car. For reasons equally obvious they had gone in Tessa's. He wondered if she had packed a suitcase, but there wasn't time to go home and look. Intent on maximum speed he disregarded Maybridge's instructions and switched on the siren. Later, after cutting through the city traffic at a steady sixty, he switched off into anonymity and listened for route instructions. Webber, he was told, was a few miles south of Stroud. If he picked up the motorway at Gloucester this was no circular tour.

Stannard calculated mileage. The Mini was elderly and the time gap was under an hour. Given reasonable conditions he could reduce it to forty minutes. Webber, under pressure, was behaving uncharacteristically. He hadn't expected this sort of confrontation with him so soon. The nature of the confrontation would be dictated by circumstances when he caught up with him. In the meantime his own emotions had to be put on ice. He didn't dare think of Tessa.

Tessa, at George's side, felt euphoric. He hadn't wanted her to come. He had wanted to drive up to Sue's parents' home on his own. He needed a car that the police wouldn't associate with him. He wanted a confrontation with Sue. They had to talk. It was necessary that they should talk alone. But Tessa had been unusually forceful, strong in her love for him. It was her car. He was welcome to it; but she was coming too. She didn't say that she would be there, cushioning the blow of defeat, taking the pain out of rejection. She didn't need to; it was implicit in her expression. The sexual act, she implied, had made them one. He could almost hear the wedding march and smell orange blossom. It was necessary to slap her down hard, but he hadn't the energy or the stomach for it. He didn't know what to do with her other than take her. He hoped she'd cool down into sanity eventually.

He wished that he, too, could behave with more normality. A rational appraisal of the situation was impossible. His mind was boiling with half-formed thoughts. What would he say—do . . . ? How would he say it . . . do it . . . ? The hot day had burned into a thundery evening, making his eyes heavy in his head. To concentrate on driving took all his energy. He wished Tessa wouldn't sit pressed up against him. What was she planning to do when Sue refused to see him? Offer him sex in the car as a consolation prize? Not possible in this tiny little box. Good. Good. A polite, perfectly understandable refusal. Then what? Elope with me . . . Fast falls the eventide . . . the evening darkens . . . love with me abide.

Why did fractured hymn tunes—scraps of blood silly doggerel—keep going through his head?

Why couldn't he think sanely—coolly?

Was he going crazy?

He overtook badly and a station-wagon hooted at him. He hooted back. Tessa laughed. She felt as if she were high on champagne. Sue wouldn't have anything to do with him. Backed by her parents she would ask him to leave. Well, that would clinch the matter. He would know exactly where he stood. I am here, she thought, loving you. Whatever the future holds, I'm beside you.

His voice was hard, cold. He told her to stop leaning on him, that she was hampering his movements. "Unless you want to get yourself killed."

The old accusation, partly forgotten, shocked her into an awareness of reality. She shivered. Her hands in her lap were cold. She wanted to open the window and breathe the night air, but she was cold. In a dilemma of indecision she rolled the window down and then up again.

He wished she would stop fidgeting. "Feeling sick?"

"No."

"If you've changed your mind about coming, I'll put you off at a service station and arrange transport back."

She believed that he was trying to spare her embarrassment and pain. "I want to be with you. You need me."

He didn't answer.

They had been on the motorway for some while now, grinding along like the high whine of a dentist's drill. His concentration wasn't good enough. He drove off at the first opportunity and took a minor road heading in the general direction of the Malvern hills. The clouds were sulphurous yellow as if the dying sun had jaundiced them in the grey bed of the sky. He crossed an intersection and the road eventually became familiar. On his last drive along it the trees had been a fresh Spring green. Sue had been at his side. Mike, in the back of the car, had been singing 'Ten Green Bottles'. Ten green bottles—five green bottles—eight green bottles. Mike couldn't count backwards.

Sue had been laughing, teasing him. Feeding him with chocolates when he got it right.

Sue, my wife.

Mike, my son.

No one—but no one—will take you from me.

It was like baying at the moon, he thought. Howling at the moon. No one had taken her from him. She had walked away . . . correction, been wheeled away . . . of her own free will.

She couldn't even walk out on me, McKendrick. She couldn't even have that dignity. At her parents' home she will be wheeled to me . . . if she wants it. Her father will hold the handles of the chair. He will present her to me. Or not.

They were getting close now. The road was narrowing and the trees were meeting overhead. He dropped speed and lowered his window. A bird had the audacity to sing. He could hear it quite clearly above the hum of the engine. He felt a thickening in his throat and swallowed convulsively a couple of times.

Tessa gently put her hand on his wrist. He suffered it, wanting savagely to tear it away.

She said, "It will be all right—you'll see." The words were intended for the future. Not for now.

The house was around the next bend and he drove very slowly, afraid of passing the entrance. The road was unlit and

169

there was little traffic. By day the manse had a certain unpretentious charm, by night it was sombre, a fit dwelling for Victorian clerics who penned joyless sermons. In these days the church was of pitch pine and the cleric was matey. Both the church and the new manse were on the new housing estate two miles away.

There were no lights.

Why were there no lights?

He got out of the car, forgetting Tessa, and slammed the door behind him.

She looked around her with growing unease. Sue had spoken to her about the beauty of the place—about the fields full of clover—about the soft mauve outline of the hills. She hadn't spoken about darkness—the smell of decaying leaves—the sound of gravel underfoot.

She opened her door and followed George, wanting to be at his side, to hold his arm, but understanding that for a while, a little while, she must hold back. This was between him and Sue, briefly, and, she hoped, not too hurtfully. After that her turn would come. She hoped the right words would occur to her. She wasn't good with words.

Her body still felt bruised. She smiled to herself in the darkness. Her image of a tender lover had been milk-pale compared with the reality. His latent violence was a facet of his character she hadn't known.

The front door was flanked by carriage lamps, now unlit. He stood under the canopy and rang the bell. The main living rooms were to the front and the kitchen and study at the back. There was a strong familiar garden smell. Mignonette? Memories, like music, whispered through his mind, but were unclear.

A few drops of thundery rain fell like flung pebbles. Tessa undid the brown silk scarf that was tucked into the neck of her sweater and put it around her head. Louis didn't like it worn that way. Irish peasant girl from the bog lands, he had described her. There was a lot about her that Louis hadn't liked. He would wave her off with some relief.

Only he wouldn't.

Where was the demarcation line between hatred and love? In her case love was non-existent, but Louis . . . ? She deliberately stopped thinking about him. It was very easy to do.

170

George was going around to the back of the house. She followed him. It didn't take him many minutes to discover that the house was empty. Sue's mother kept the spare key under a flower-pot in the greenhouse. He fumbled about for it in the darkness and eventually found it. He had told her many times that it was a stupid place to keep it, but she had merely smiled at him. He and Sue's mother had got on well. Under these circumstances, though, could he count on her goodwill? Probably not. He wondered how much she had been told. Sue's father would be only too happy to kick him to hell. A murder suspect could be legitimately savaged. How much would Sue stand for? How much could she stand? Where had they taken her? Out for a drink, perhaps? The local down in the village was genuine sixteenth century—unspoiled. They had spent many an evening there in the past in the days when he was courting Sue. Courting? An old-fashioned word. An old-fashioned girl. They hadn't slept together until their wedding night.

Tessa said, "They're out," and moved closer to him. The dark house and garden frightened her.

He frowned down at her, aware that she looked different, and then he realised that she had put a scarf around her head. It pressed her hair down and made her face look thin. He imagined what she would look like in middle-age. A neat, faded little woman, meticulously tidy—like her house. Her shining, neat little house.

He unlocked the back door and switched on the kitchen light. The kitchen paper, bunches of cherries on a white background, seemed to screech a cheerful welcome.

Tessa observed truthfully, "It's in appalling taste."

He agreed. He liked Sue's mother, but her choice of kitchen paper was indefensible. A conversation about taste—sartorial—decorative—or whathaveyou—would be pleasantly banal and soothing. He hoped Tessa would expand her opinion. He smiled at her encouragingly.

She looked at him, startled, and didn't smile back.

He suggested that they should go through to the drawing room and wait. "They probably won't be long. At this hour of the evening they sometimes go to the village for a drink."

He was speaking very calmly—unnaturally calmly, she thought.

She asked him if he were feeling all right.

The question surprised him. All right? All wrong? A mixture of the two. His head felt light as if it belonged to someone else.

He told her he felt adequate, and the answer silenced her as she pondered it.

Adequate? For what?

The drawing-room paper was a blue trellis and the carpet a blue and white Indian. Over the cream marble fireplace was a painting of Sue when she was a little girl. She was about eight and her hair was in two heavy plaits. Her eyes were questioning and her lips faintly smiled. The future is going to be gorgeous, her expression implied. Well, it is, isn't it? *Isn't* it?

George stood looking up at it. Mike had inherited her expression of rather uncertain optimism.

Tessa asked if she might switch on the electric heater. The room, despite its cosiness, which she rather liked, was chill.

"Of course." He switched on the double bar. "Would you like some coffee while we wait?"

Yes, she would like some coffee, but having made the suggestion he didn't follow it through and it seemed presumptuous to make it herself. Sue's parents might object to a stranger in the kitchen. She felt very much a stranger now, or rather worse—an intruder. Of course she had no business being here, but she didn't regret having come.

George was roaming around the room restlessly, picking up pieces of bric-a-brac like a thief assessing values. She said, mainly to break the silence, that Sue's mother had nice things.

"Nice," he agreed. "Yes, very nice." Small things, pretty things, your sort of things.

He returned to the fireplace and sat opposite her in a wine coloured velvet armchair. "Tessa."

"Yes?"

"Take your scarf off."

She had forgotten that it was still around her head. She loosened it and draped it over her shoulders.

"That's better," he approved. "Much better."

He began smiling again and the smile filled her with unease. She looked away from him and at the fingers curled gently in her lap.

The clock on the mantelpiece had a loud tick and when it

172

reached the half hour it struck a single clear note. Time, George thought, is important. Time, according to Maybridge, is very important. The questions of the inquisition began churning through his head again. How long walking, sitting, thinking, raping, strangling, going home? Ten minutes, twenty minutes, thirty minutes, forty? His wristwatch was three minutes fast. He adjusted it.

They had been in the house now for nearly half an hour.

Twenty-two

STANNARD MET NAYLOR AT THE CROSSROADS NEAR THE manse and listened while Naylor gave him careful directions. "It's easy to miss, sir. I'd come with you, only I've orders to stay in the car."

Maybridge being tactful, Stannard thought, but he was past being grateful for anything. He drove his car to the bottom of the drive and left it there while he walked around the building. As a bolt-hole the house was conveniently remote. He wondered if Tessa had been here with Webber before. The drawing-room curtains were drawn back and he could see her and Webber sitting at opposite sides of the fireplace. Sitting decorously, not even talking.

On the evenings when he and Tessa had sat together—as she and Webber were sitting now—they had made conversational jabs at each other, little more. Their silences had been *lacunae* of nervous tension. Intellectually he matched her, was possibly her superior, but he had no gift for expressing his thoughts. Sexually, too, he was clumsy. Foreplay had never been any part of his approach. He wasn't of the Webber breed. He lacked his education—his smoothness—his bloody style.

That Tessa should succumb to Webber's blandishments wasn't surprising. As he watched them he was filled with deep bitterness. Once Webber had started trespassing on his patch Tessa's withdrawal from him had begun. A memory of their wedding day came to him. She had worn a cream-coloured dress and had been able to laugh enough in those days to call it semi-virginal. She had laughed very little since. *Except with Webber*. Shared laughter. Shared silence. Shared bed.

In the early days he had tried to become what she wanted him to be, but the image was too impossibly romantic. He couldn't change to that degree. In time he had stopped trying.

Webber didn't have to try.

Webber just sat there.

Tessa just sat there—looking at him.

Watching Tessa watching Webber made his anger almost uncontrollable. He imagined Webber dead. It was a good image and he savoured it. But when he rang the doorbell and George opened the door to him the greeting on both sides was mild.

Tessa, tensed for the moment of meeting Sue and her parents, relaxed a little at what she saw as a lesser trauma. Louis, she supposed, in the guise of watchdog, had come to haul George back to within acceptable police limits. A five-mile radius of the city centre, perhaps? The fact that the time to make her own statement of intent had arrived dawned on her slowly. George, withdrawn, non-communicative, had been sitting in silence while she had tried to prepare him for his meeting with Sue. Sue would appreciate his having made the journey, she said. The meeting would have taken place sooner or later: better sooner. Physically maimed as she was, Sue couldn't be expected to have emotional strength. One sapped the other.

His expression had halted her. She realised that she was choosing the wrong words and had better be silent.

Totally concerned for him she had forgotten Louis completely, and had relegated her own showdown to the back of her mind; and now Louis was here.

His masculinity—raw—brutal—even when dressed up in his less than immaculate working clothes offended her. She remembered George naked and made the comparison. In an unguarded moment she looked directly at Louis and he saw the contempt in her eyes as he had seen it many times before.

The veins in his forehead felt like threads of fire.

He addressed her harshly. "Having a pleasant time?"

She was cool, composed, not placatory. "Very."

"Where the hell were you going? Some cosy little cot in the Highlands—or across the sea to your bloody Ireland? Peat digs easily, I'm told. He'd have no sweat burying you."

"Don't talk like a fool."

"He's a murder suspect."

"You don't have to remind me of that idiocy." The extent of her faith in Webber shone out clearly. He knew that there she was unshakable.

He turned and looked at Webber. "You were told not to leave the city without permission."

Webber seemed amused. "I have been told many things in my time. Not all of them made sense."

"If it's not too indelicate a question, what are your immediate plans for my wife?"

George, feeling like a prisoner released from a strait-jacket, walked over to the drinks cabinet and poured himself a whisky. "To return her to you so that you may drive her back. Your coming here is opportune—provided you don't stay." The whisky was strong and heartening. He swallowed it with pleasure.

He turned back to Stannard. "I'm here to meet Sue. She returned here earlier today—with her parents. This is her parents' home. I have to speak to her so I borrowed Tessa's car—in case your lot tried to block the meeting. Tessa accompanied me out of kindness."

Stannard didn't believe it. "You're telling me your wife is on the premises?"

'Your wife'. Very formal.

Once, not so long ago, George thought, you trod on Mike's toy car in the kitchen. You promised him another one. You didn't keep your promise. It was an odd irrelevancy, as if the normal edged in on the abnormal as a reminder that life wasn't always like this.

"No, Sue's not here. I expect her to be here soon."

"Where is she now?"

George shrugged. "Possibly having a drink in the village with her parents. I don't know." He interpreted Stannard's expression correctly. "If I were lying," he pointed out, "I could do much better."

Tessa said quietly, "Sue couldn't take the hounding—the insinuations. The brick through the window was more than she could stand. He's here to try to persuade her to go home with

176

him. She won't go. Any more than I will go with you." The words were cold—very final.

She got up and went over to stand beside George. "I'm not going back with Louis," she told him. "You said I came out of kindness. I didn't. If you're sending me back out of kindness, then don't. I can't help the way I feel about you. I can't hide it."

No, Stannard thought, you can't hide it. You never could. But Webber can hide it—too bloody well he can hide it.

"You've fucked her, of course?"

George didn't answer. All this was an embarrassing intrusion—a nuisance. None of it mattered. It was necessary that they should go away—both of them—before Sue came. He was aware of Stannard's anger, but it didn't touch him. He was aware, too, of Tessa's pain, but was too bludgeoned by his own to be able to respond.

It was Tessa who answered. Hatred, pure and simple, shone from her eyes. "Not in your sense—no. We loved physically. There's a difference." She looked at George, waiting for emotional support. None came.

She poured herself a small measure of whisky and took it over to the sofa and sat down. She couldn't hold the glass steady and drops of the drink splashed on to her hands. She put the glass down in the hearth. The clock was ticking very loudly, throbbing into the silence like a heart beat. Her mind began seeking out reasons for George's attitude. His break with Sue was like losing a limb. He had loved her for a long time. All right—so he couldn't make the move into her bed that fast. She could accept it. She could wait. There were times tonight when she believed him to be on the verge of a breakdown. It wasn't surprising considering the treatment he had had. He was sensitive, imaginative. He had been hounded into the ground. He didn't have a proper grasp on reality. Half the time he had talked about inconsequential matters and smiled as if they amused him. The rest of the time when she had tried to guide his thoughts into the future—to make sensible plans—he had become edgy and morose. He was a man of deep feeling. He needed to get away for a while, perhaps on his own. He needed to think calmly. Tonight he wasn't calm. Far from it.

Neither was she. If she couldn't be with him now then she

couldn't be with anybody. She couldn't go back to her house again—not even to pick up her clothes. Louis's presence made her feel sick. She had enough money on her to spend one night at a hotel—somewhere—anywhere. After that she would move in with one of her friends at the hospital—temporarily, until she could find a room for herself. In a while—a week or so—George would have adjusted to losing Sue. They would be able to talk together. To make plans for the future. She had been precipitate this evening. It wasn't his fault. It was hers. She wanted to lie in his arms again. She was longing to have him inside her again. Her skin crawled with desire for him. She lacked his control. He had arranged his priorities and Sue came first. Tonight Sue came first. Afterwards . . .

She spoke to him directly. "You know I love you."

"Tessa—I'm sorry." There was an edge of exasperation in his voice. He tried to level it out, but it was there.

Stannard touched her on the shoulder. "My car is at the bottom of the drive. Leave yours here. Webber can return it later."

At this stage he had no power to arrest Webber. Let the bastard stay here. It didn't matter. He was behaving very calmly towards him under the circumstances. Very professionally. He congratulated himself on his restraint. Sweat, sour and profuse, was bathing his body. He wondered if Tessa could smell it.

She was sitting in a half-hoop of pain, her arms around her stomach. He knew the feeling.

He spoke her name with some gentleness. "Tessa?"

She raised her head and looked at him. He was gross—repulsive.

She told him so.

It was at that point that he finally lost control. She had gone panting around Webber like a bitch in heat and he had taken her without even the slightest vestige of feeling for her. Love—a stupid word. It was a knife ripping your balls. It was a corrosive poison in your gut that sent you out into the darkness looking for—what? Sexual relief? Acts of bestiality as a form of revenge on the women who were not Tessa. The memories began crowding back into his mind. He began reliving it all, walking through the darkness again, shaking with excitement and a sick kind of joy.

At the end of the darkness was Webber. He had gone over to

178

the mantelpiece and was leaning up against it under the painting of a child with long, dark hair. He was saying something to Tessa—reproving her for what she had said. His voice was cool—faintly supercilious—carefully unamused. He was looking at her and she at him.

And then he turned and saw the gun.

He made a protesting movement with his hands in which there was more surprise than fear.

Stannard waited a couple of seconds for the fear to come and then he raised the Webley and fired. He had been carrying it for some while now and could normally shoot with precision. Cold, unemotional target practice was one thing—anger-motivated killing was another. The bullet grazed Webber's skull, fracturing it, and then sped on and embedded itself in the portrait. The air reverberated with the noise of the gunshot and the crashing of a tableful of bric-a-brac as Webber staggered against it. He lurched forward and then slumped over a wine-coloured chair, pitching it over on to its side. A chair the colour of blood. Appropriate. His head was half-buried by one of the cushions and he was bleeding into it. A botched killing. Not clean. Death by gunshot seldom was. It would be a kindness to pump a second bullet into him and finish him fast. But why be kind?

Stannard turned to Tessa, wondering why she was so silent. Why wasn't she tearing at him? Why wasn't she weeping and making all the noises of the newly bereaved? Why wasn't she wiping away Webber's blood with her dainty little handkerchief?

She was sitting like a small, cold statue on the sofa—unmoving. Her hands were clenched at her side. And then she began to shake—slow tremors—regular, like the pangs of parturition—swept over her.

He said coldly, "It had to be done. He used you. Felt nothing for you. Flung you back at me."

He looked at her glazed eyes and felt some compassion for her. Her death wouldn't be like the other deaths. He would do nothing to shame her. Neither would it be by gun. There would be no rupturing of flesh. No blemish. The scarf around her neck. A quick twist.

He took it gently from around her shoulders and fingered it.

179

Brown silk with small white flowers on it. He had given it to her on her last birthday together with a flower pendant. He thought she would have liked the pendant—a small pearl surrounded with tiny leaves of gold. It was pretty. It had cost a lot. She hadn't even tried it on, just thanked him and put it in her jewel box. That night her suffering of the sexual act had been more than usually overt. Later that same night he had gone out and done his first killing—Nurse Gray. It had been very easy. Very satisfying. McKendrick's daughter had been less easy; she had made for his eyes and kneed him in the groin. Less easy, but even more satisfying. The contest had been stimulating. The Brand woman, despite her weight and size, had been the weakest of the three. There had been less pleasure in that one. There was no bloom of youth there. The flesh was slack and ageing.

Not sweet and young.

Your throat is like silk, Tessa.

Why do you sit there so still?

Why aren't your eyes looking into mine?

I can feel your heart beating. You're not shaking anymore. Not frightened anymore? No resistance? No fear? Why?

Tessa, damn you—*react*!

The scarf is around your throat. I'm about to tighten it. Why don't you scream—fight—give me some sort of impetus?

He was aware of the limpness in his hands as if the nerves refused to activate the fingers. He had drowned a kitten once—it had scratched and bitten. Had it stayed still and docile he couldn't have done it. The small, the fragile, the helpless—they each had a certain immunity.

She was sitting there. Accepting death. Her eyes gazing beyond him at Webber.

He hadn't cried since boyhood, but he was crying now as he stepped away from her. She made a small movement as the scarf slackened and drifted to the floor and her breath came painfully.

Still she didn't look at him.

She hadn't seen his tears, and for that he was glad.

He picked up the gun from the chair where he had placed it and looked over at Webber. His skin was grey. There were

180

traces of blood on the carpet now—dark smudges on the deep pile.

He didn't glance at Tessa again.

He went out into the hall and opened the front door. As the night air, crisp and clean, touched his face, his muscles stiffened into control.

He saw that Naylor had driven to the bottom of the drive and parked behind his car. Maybridge was there, too. Obviously they hadn't heard the gunshot or they would have been up here before now. But they would come to investigate the situation soon. Had he succeeded in killing Tessa he could have said that Webber had strangled her and that he had shot him. The scenario had refused to be played.

A scenario in which he served a life-sentence for the murder of Webber and—if they dug out the truth—the others, would not be played either.

I cried for you, Tessa, you uncaring little bitch. I'm not going to spend a lifetime in prison for you.

There was no point in going on with any of it. No valid reason for survival. He had reached the bottom of the pit a few minutes ago. It took too much energy to try to crawl out of it—to crawl out of it into a desolate landscape offering nothing.

He closed the door and went back through the house to the kitchen. He poured himself a glass of water at the sink and stood looking out at the moonlit back garden. There was a copse of trees at the bottom of it. They gave privacy. He couldn't possibly do what he was about to do in the garish little kitchen and within earshot of Tessa. Let the others find him— not Tessa. Not that she would care if she did find him. It was necessary to hang on to that particular truth.

And not start weeping about it again.

Just accept it.

She wouldn't care.

It didn't matter.

Nothing mattered.

He had disposed of Webber clumsily. His own death would be efficient. It would also have the virtue of being fast.

He walked down the moss-covered path through the vegetable garden and reached the deeper darkness of the trees and then lay down in the embracing, sinewy arms of superficial roots.

He wished he could lie there for a long time, smelling the wet leaves, the tang of the earth. Sleep for a while, perhaps, and then awake to something different. A world in which the sun shone. It had been a hell of a marriage. Cold little Saint Theresa. Contemptuous little Saint Theresa. Pretty little body. Soft, cold flesh. Eyes full of hate.

The gun was hard between his teeth. Death tasted of metal. It was phallic. He thought fleetingly of the three dead women—particularly of Harriet Brand. She, too, had died in a garden shaded by trees. Hers had been the only planned killing. It was the only time he had tailed Webber and used his presence in the vicinity to commit murder in cold blood. Had Maybridge not sent him out in pursuit of Webber tonight Webber might have been convicted on circumstantial evidence—had further evidence been planted. He had failed to plant it in time.

Failure meant a long sleep.

To hell with euphemisms.

Failure meant total darkness. An end.

Twenty-three

"I BEHAVED UNPROFESSIONALLY BY TELLING YOU," REND-come said to McKendrick. "But you had to be told. There's a time for discretion and it isn't now. Later—after the laboratory tests—I'll divulge his name to the Press." He added, "He's dead—perhaps fortunately under the circumstances."

It was the early hours of the morning and Webber was due for immediate surgery. Rendcome had waylaid McKendrick on his way to the theatre and they were talking together in the hospital corridor. "The case is still to be proved," he went on. "It will be. You must take my word for it."

Twenty-four hours of tests would, he knew, clinch it. Stannard's wife, in a state of shock, but sufficiently coherent to show them the broad outline of what had happened, was now under sedation. A chance remark, made in great bitterness, about the withholding of the violin had given Maybridge the lead he needed. Webber's violin, still at police headquarters, had been cleared of incriminating evidence. Stannard's violin, possibly bought as a thespian gesture and used during the Harriet Brand killing, would be tested forensically. On phoned instructions from Maybridge, Stannard's shed had been thoroughly searched. Clothes, worn very probably during the killings, had been found under the floorboards, together with a blue silk scarf. Particles of blue silk had been found in the mouths of the three victims. The clothes and the scarf would be tested for saliva and semen and the results were already a foregone conclusion.

It was odd that Stannard hadn't been able to kill his wife.
Or was it?

In his role of many years as Chief Constable Rendcome had learnt not to be too surprised by anything.

In the meantime Webber's innocence had to be underlined. So he underlined it.

He didn't say in so many words that Paul, together with Rachel Gray and Ian Mavor, might behave unethically. There would be no culpable negligence. Webber's life was in the hands of his three main accusers and they would fight harder to save it now that he was no longer a murder suspect. Well—they were human.

Paul said crisply, "You've made your point."

He could still lose Webber. The skull X-ray showed a linear fracture on the right side crossing the middle meningeal artery. It was fortunate the bullet hadn't penetrated.

He had no time for further talk with Rendcome, but he had to make time to pass the message along to the other two. What did Rendcome think they were—three ghouls who would have taken vengeance had the situation been different? The idea angered him. Had he been able to repress disturbing memories of his earlier attitude to Webber, he would have listened to Rendcome with amusement. It was salutary to have one's darker side pushed into the glare of truth. He was glad Webber was in the clear—glad for his own peace of mind at this particular moment. He would do all he could for him.

Gowned and scrubbed, Ian and Rachel listened to him, much as he had listened to Rendcome, but in the girl he sensed a deeper underlying distress. Her eyes slid away from him almost guiltily and she looked at Ian—for comfort? What was the matter with her—a guilt complex? Yes, probably. Most of the rumours had started there. Well, if she wanted to expiate anything she could do it by assisting to the best of her skill.

As the operation progressed he became totally professional and impersonal, unaware of anything other than the fact that the bleeding was copious and had to be controlled. The torn middle meningeal artery was the source of the blood loss. He located it eventually and clipped it. Replacing the bone flap and skin caused no problem. Despite the haemorrhaging Webber would survive. By tomorrow his level of consciousness might well be normal.

Memory of Webber's impassioned rejection of his skill—his 'goddamned healing hands', as he called them—came to him suddenly. Well, they hadn't been so useless this time—and thank God for it. It could easily have gone the other way.

He looked tiredly at his anaesthetist and nodded his satisfaction and his thanks.

Harriet, you would have done well, too.

He tried not to think of her.

The sun would soon be up. The operation had taken a long time. The young ones looked less tired than he felt, but even so the strain showed. He sensed their mutual support as they looked at each other, and resented it.

Maggie, I'm still jealous for you. I shouldn't be. I can't help it.

You went on loving people.

It was fortunate for Webber that he had Sue. She was waiting in the visitors' room for news. He decided to deliver it personally.

She looked small and pinched and cold, despite the warmth of the room. Someone—her mother, probably—had put a second cardigan over her shoulders and the sleeves dangled over the wheels of her chair. He acknowledged her parents briefly and then told her quickly what she needed to know.

"You can stop worrying. Had the bullet penetrated it might have been a different story. In a few hours you'll be able to see him. You can be around when he wakes up."

She began weeping with relief. The anxiety had been agonising; she had never known such despairing pain in her life.

Paul said gently, "He'll be weak for a while. He'll need your care."

"I'll give it." (Humbly, gratefully, with delight, I'll give it.)

He touched her hand. "Yes," he said, "I know."

It would be a reversal of the roles—not for long, but for long enough to be therapeutic for both of them.

As he went down to his car Rendcome caught up with him. He answered his unspoken question. "He'll be okay."

"Good."

And Stannard's wife, Rendcome thought, what of her? What sort of medication will get her back on her feet? According to the cliché, time healed. Clichés were often right. She was young. The young were more emotionally vulnerable than the old, but the pain, though sharper, tended not to last. He wondered if she would return to Ireland. It would perhaps be the best thing for her to do.

And then he stopped thinking about her and began savouring the golden, autumnal air.

It was a nice morning. Very early. Very innocent.

The day with its problems, its ugly moments and its good ones, was waiting in the wings. Three murders had been solved. Just now the stage was empty and very pleasant. He suggested to Paul that he might like to drive home across the Downs. He had come to the hospital in one of the police cars and someone else could see to that. Police matters—for a while—could be forgotten.

"And then come in and have breakfast with us."

It was a good end to a difficult night. A good start to an unpredictable day.

Paul accepted.

About the Author

B.M. Gill is also the author of DEATH DROP and THE TWELFTH JUROR. Formerly a teacher, she now writes full-time from her home in a village in Wales.

MURDER...
MAYHEM...
MYSTERY...

From Ballantine